Friends

OF

LAFAYETTE LIBRARY
AND LEARNING CENTER

generously provided

this book

WHEN REAL PIGEONS GET SPLASHED...

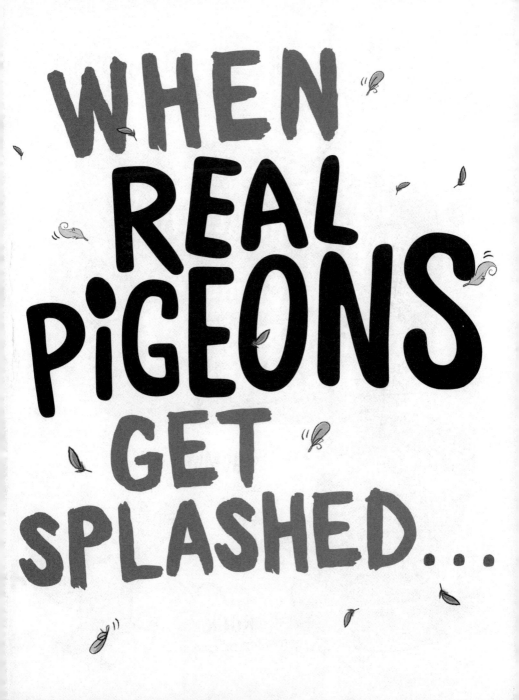

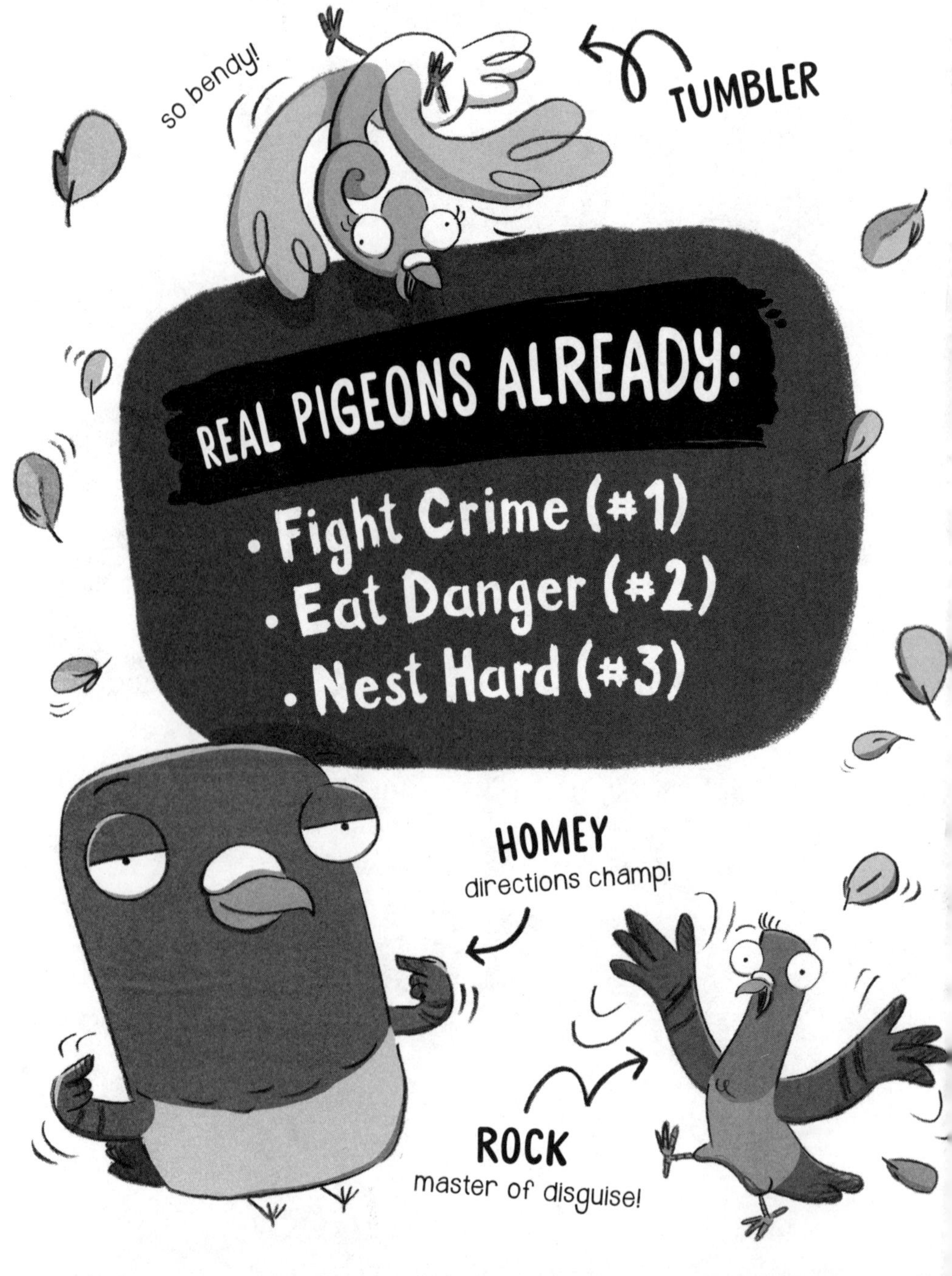
so bendy!
TUMBLER
REAL PIGEONS ALREADY:
• Fight Crime (#1)
• Eat Danger (#2)
• Nest Hard (#3)
HOMEY
directions champ!
ROCK
master of disguise!

REAL PIGEONS

4

SPLASH BACK

WITHDRAWN

FRILLBACK
superstrong!

RANDOM HOUSE NEW YORK

ANDREW McDONALD and BEN WOOD

CONTENTS

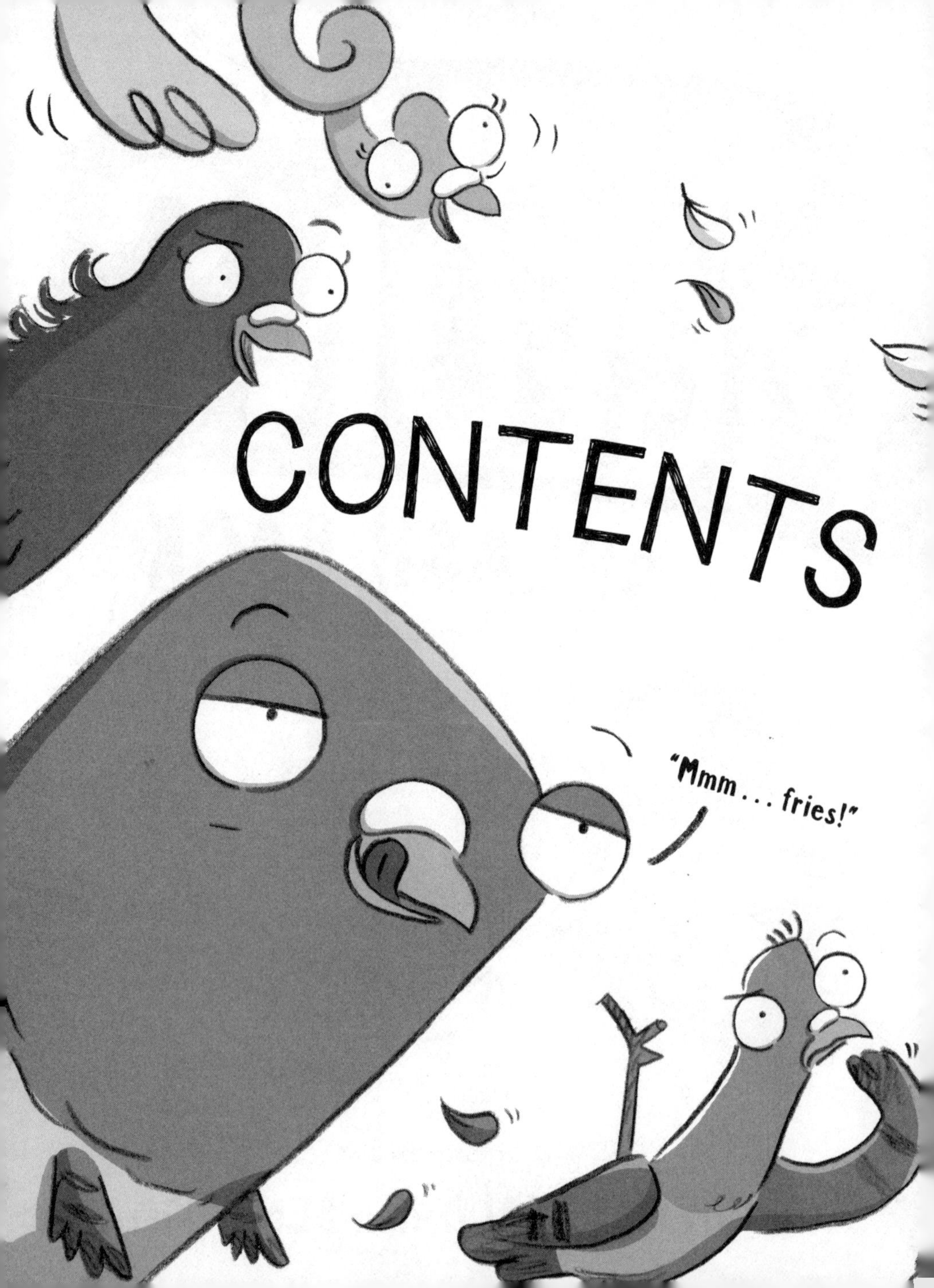
"Mmm . . . fries!"

FOR ELISE —ANDREW

FOR JOHN —BEN

Text copyright © 2019 by Andrew McDonald
Cover art and interior illustrations copyright © 2019 by Ben Wood
Series design copyright © 2019 by Hardie Grant Children's Publishing

All rights reserved. Published in the United States by Random House Children's Books, a division of Penguin Random House LLC, New York. Originally published in paperback by Hardie Grant Children's Publishing, Australia, in 2019.

Random House and the colophon are registered trademarks of Penguin Random House LLC.

Visit us on the Web! rhcbooks.com

Educators and librarians, for a variety of teaching tools, visit us at RHTeachersLibrarians.com

Library of Congress Cataloging-in-Publication Data is available upon request.
ISBN 978-0-593-42716-3 (hc) — ISBN 978-0-593-42717-0 (lib. bdg.) — ISBN 978-0-593-42718-7 (ebook)

Printed in the United States of America

10 9 8 7 6 5 4 3 2 1

First American Edition 2021

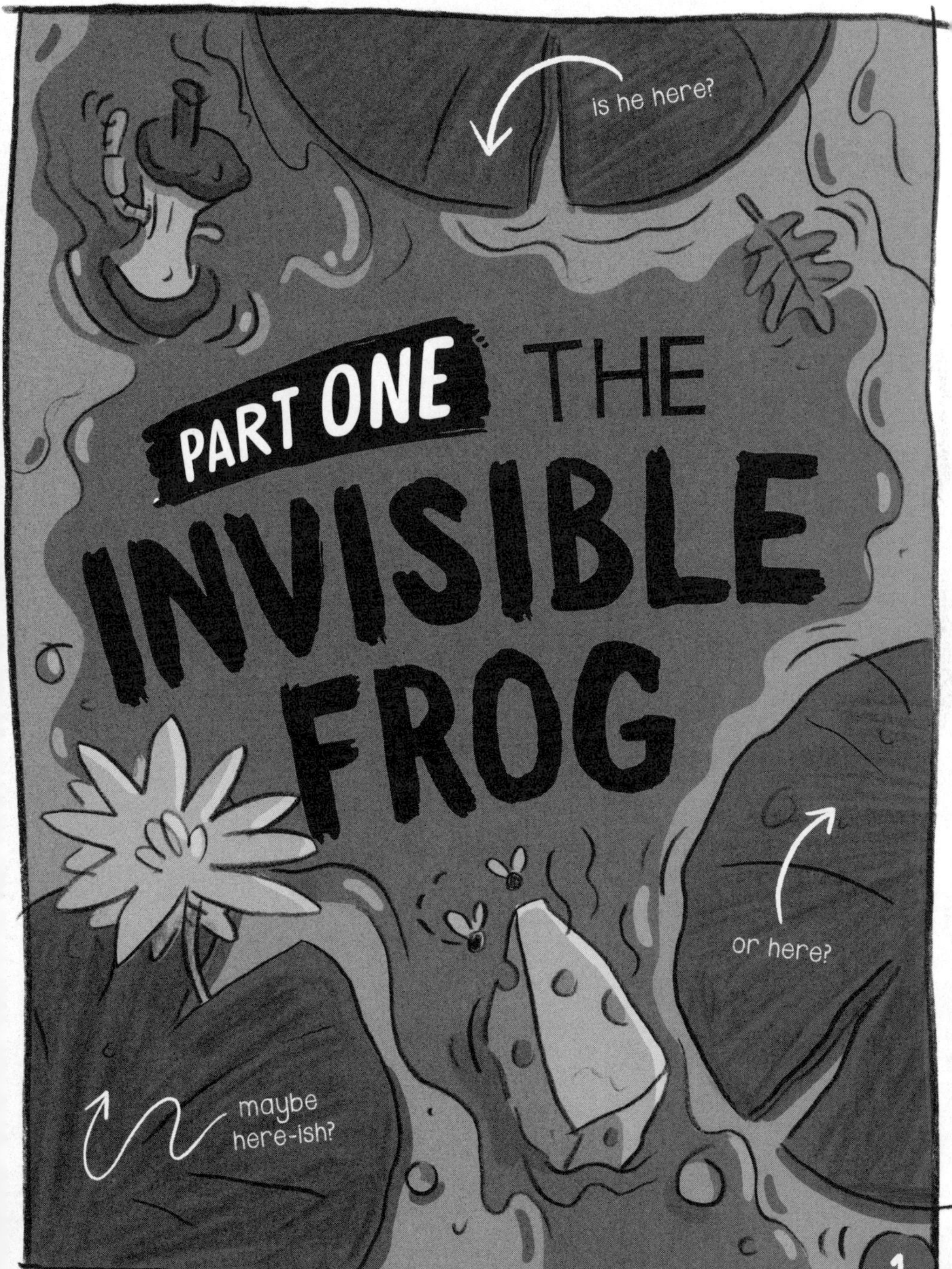
is he here?
PART ONE
THE INVISIBLE FROG
or here?
maybe here-ish?

CHAPTER 1

Which of these things would **NEVER** happen?

A pigeon singing opera.

"LA! LA! LA!"

A pigeon and a dinosaur having a sword fight.

Or a pigeon going for a swim?

That's right—**ALL** these things are **impossible.** Especially a pigeon going for a swim!

PIGEONS

(not suitable for swimming)

doesn't know what backstroke is

has beak, not gills

legs too short

feet not webbed

Pigeons can't even dog-paddle.

But they can . . .

FLOAT!

SPLASH!

SOAK!

AND DRINK!

"This water tastes like bird feet!"

This is Rock Pigeon.

He and his friends are in a crime-fighting squad called the **REAL PIGEONS.**

Protecting the city can be dirty work. So the squad has flown to a big water fountain in the park for a bath. Baths are usually very relaxing.

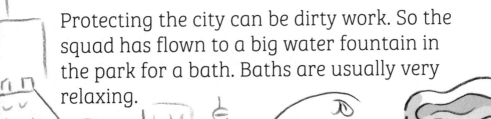

"I'm a cannonball!"

SPLASH!

"Careful, Tumbler!" says Grandpouter.

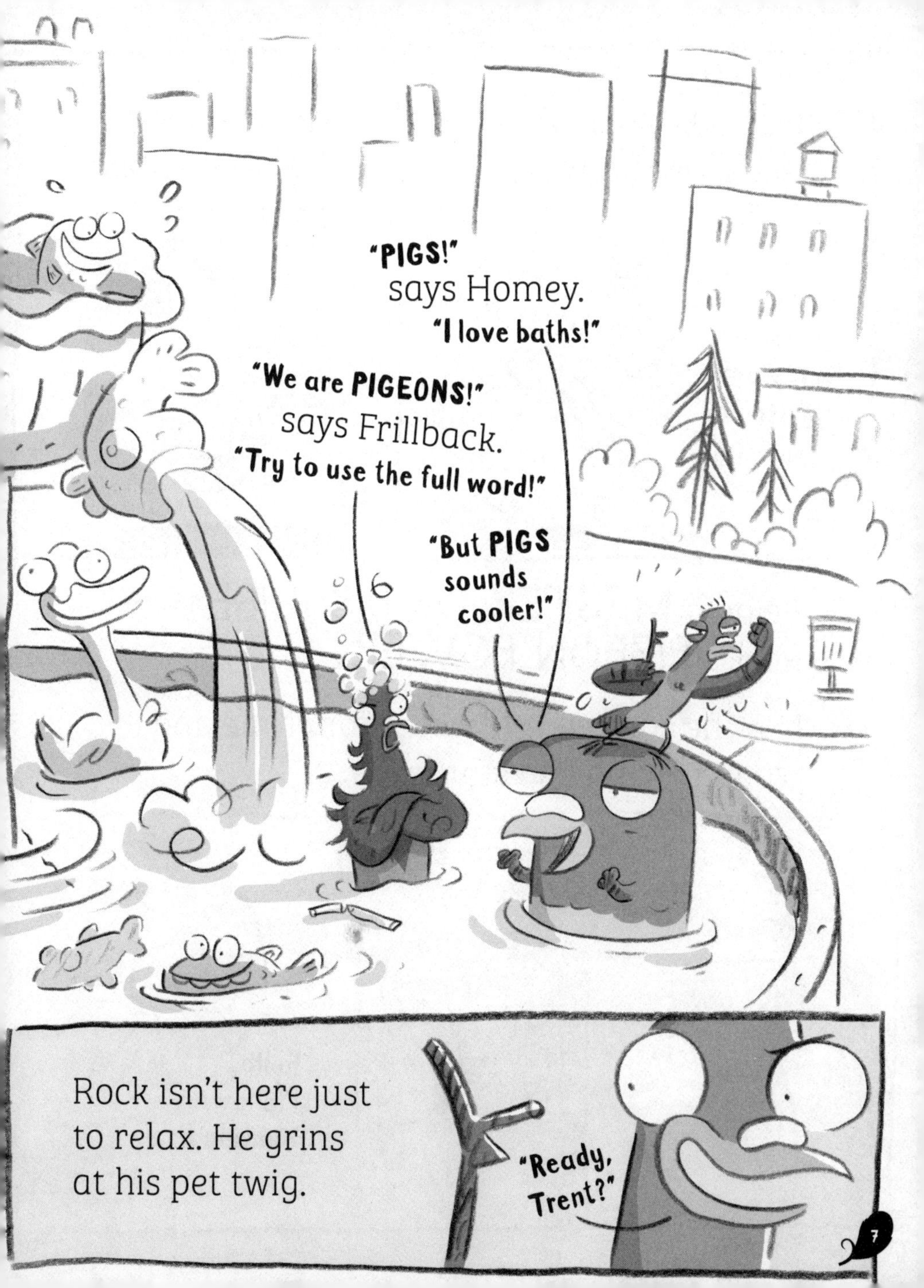

"PIGS!" says Homey.
"I love baths!"
"We are PIGEONS!" says Frillback.
"Try to use the full word!"
"But PIGS sounds cooler!"
Rock isn't here just to relax. He grins at his pet twig.
"Ready, Trent?"

He finds a ball of foil under his wing.

"I knew this would be useful one day!"

He wraps the foil around his body.

Being a **MASTER OF DISGUISE** is Rock's **PIGEON POWER.**

Now he can secretly watch for crime and trouble—as a fish statue!

"Hello, fellow fountain fish!"

Rock squirts a goldfish that is nibbling bird bottoms.

"OW!"

He squirts a duckling to stop her from falling into the fountain.

"Wheee!"

"My baby!"

And he squirts Tumbler, who keeps splashing other birds.

"There will be no water left if you keep doing that!"

"Sorry! I just love being a cannonball!"

Suddenly, a bird swoops down from the sky.

"Thank goodness I found you, young pigeons!"

It's Homey's dad, **Homer.**

"DAD-PIG!" says Homey. "What are you doing here?"

"I came because I had a vision of the future," says Homer, landing on the fountain. "You are all in DANGER!"

"Whaaaat?!"

Getting visions is Homer's PIGEON POWER.

"In my vision, I saw an UNDERGROUND MONSTER nearby," Homer explains. "It is about to cause UNTOLD MAYHEM. Something to do with water!"

"What does that have to do with us?" asks Rock. "We live aboveground!"

But at that moment . . .

. . . water starts disappearing from the fountain!

In the blink of an eye, it all drains away and the fountain is suddenly **EMPTY.**

"It seems the **UNDERGROUND MONSTER** has stolen our water," cries Grandpouter. "Homer was right!"

"I'll get to the bottom of this," declares Tumbler, and she dives into the drain.

Tumbler glides easily through the pipes under the city.

She doesn't find the vanished water. Or the **UNDERGROUND MONSTER.** But she does make other discoveries.

"Water has been stolen from birdbaths," she cries.

"And from human baths!"

"And even from public swimming pools!"

"I can finally touch the bottom!"

Tumbler finds the squad again.

"Bad news," she says. "Water has disappeared from **EVERYWHERE!**"

The mystery of the missing water is a citywide emergency.

"What are we going to do?"

"We can't buy bottled water. Because ducks don't have money!"

"Maybe we should leave the city and look for water elsewhere?"

"Don't panic, everyone!" says Rock.

"Yes, that's what we'll do!"

"PANIC!"

"There's no need for that," says Grandpouter, shaking his head. "Squad, we just found a new case!"

"REAL PIGEONS FIND MISSING WATER!"

"One last thing," says Homer. "I had **ANOTHER** vision. About the **REAL PIGEONS** squad ending!"

The pigeons are stunned.

"Noooo!" whimpers Rock.

"The squad can't end," says Tumbler, sadly. "I don't want to go back to my old job of plugging holes in trees so squirrels don't catch colds!"

"**HOW** will the squad end?" asks Grandpouter.

"All I know is that **SOMEONE** will end it," says Homer. "I don't know who or how. But my visions always come true."

Rock gulps.

There are lots of ways the squad could end.

A villain could slingshot them into space.

"HELP!"

"HA HA HA!"

Or a cat could eat them for an ap-pig-tizer.

"Yum! Yum! Yum!"

Or Rock could turn evil—and become a **BAD BIRD.**

"And I thought I was trouble!"

Rock shivers when he thinks about the squad ending.

But then he straightens out his feathers.

He points Trent at the sky.

And loudly declares, "I will protect us! No one is going to end the **REAL PIGEONS** squad while I'm around!"

"Right now you've got an **UNDERGROUND MONSTER** to worry about," says Homer, taking flight. "And I just had another vision— of myself eating breakfast! Goodbye and good luck, **REAL PIGLETS!**"

"We'd better head **UNDERGROUND,**" says Grandpouter. "That's where the water went. And it's where the **MONSTER** must be."

"This is so serious I don't even feel like eating a **BREAD CRUMB!**" says Homey.

"But I will anyway!"

The pigeons stare nervously down into a sewer.

The underground looks scary.

But Rock said he would keep the squad safe. So he finds an unused match and jumps down.

"Come on, squad!"

And he tries not to think about the
UNDERGROUND MONSTER!

CHAPTER 2

The pigeons land in the sewer under the city.

Rock passes Trent to Frillback and lights the match.

"I don't want Trent accidentally catching fire!"

"I've got you, Trent!"

The ground is sticky. It is **EERILY** quiet. The walls are covered in slime.

"Slime is the sweat of the city!"

"I'm more worried about rats."

But there is no water to be seen.

"Stay close, squad," says Rock as they walk along the sewer. "I won't let anyone end the **REAL PIGEONS.**"

"How will you protect us **ALL, Rock?**"

But then a worm floats by.

"Is that a . . . **GHOST WORM?**"

cries Homey.

The pigeons scream. **"AAHHHH HH!"**

24

Whenever pigeons get scared, their **PIGEON INSTINCT** is to fly upward. Toward the sky. But there is no sky underground.

At that moment, something magically appears around the worm.

It's a . . .

. . . FROG!

"I must have hit my head harder than I thought!"

The frog eats the worm.

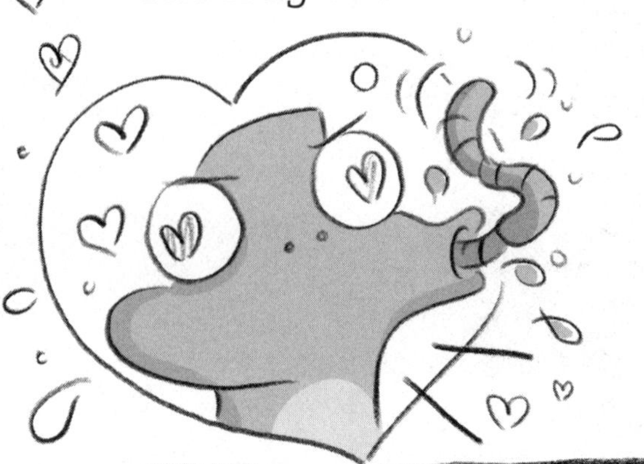

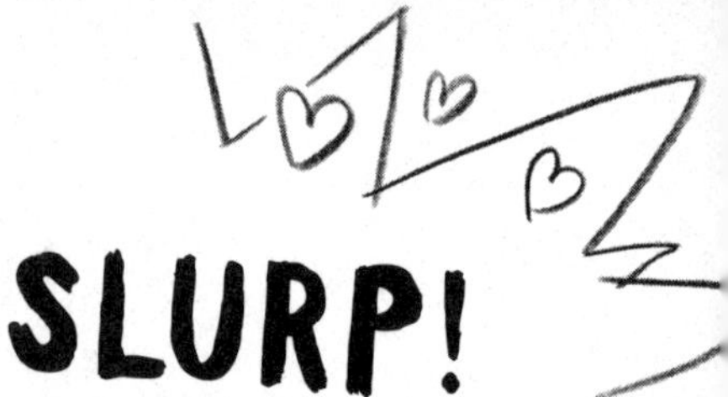
SLURP!

"We thought that worm was a ghost!" says Rock.

"You sweet, silly birds!" The frog smiles. "There's no such thing as ghosts."

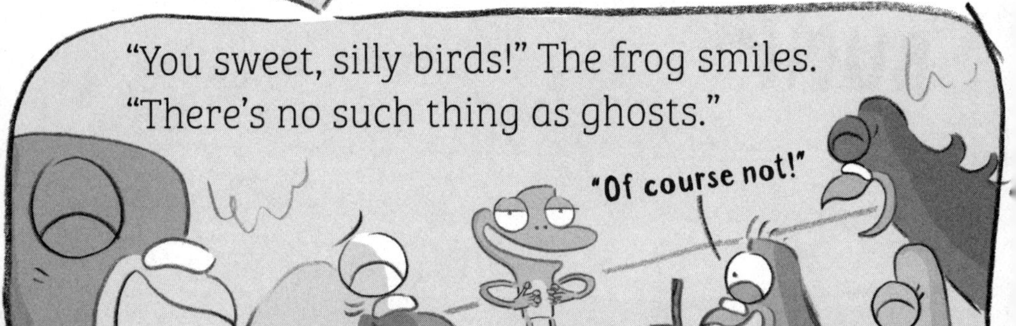
"Of course not!"

"But I *can* turn myself INVISIBLE!" the frog adds.

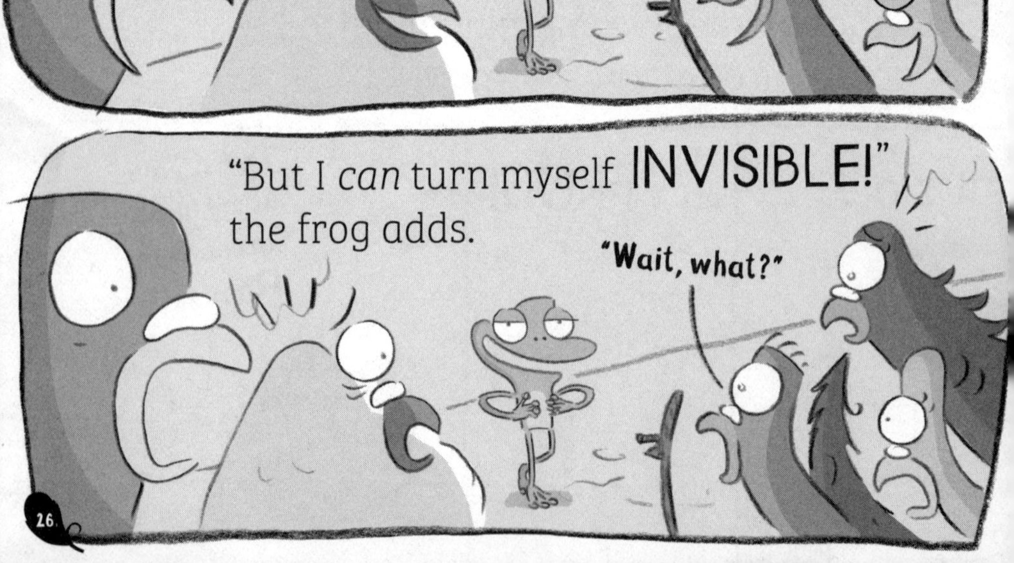
"Wait, what?"

"I am a **Gray Tree Frog.**" He grins. "I can blend into backgrounds. Watch this!"

"That's why my name is **InvisiFrog,**" he cries. "And you are beautiful birds! You really make the color gray work for you."

"He's invisible AND charming!"

The pigeons blush.

"Are you movie stars? Or models?"

"We are the **REAL PIGEONS,**" says Rock. "We're crime-fighters, investigating the city's **MISSING WATER.**"

"Get out!" cries **InvisiFrog.** "I'm a crime-fighter too! Jump onto my lily pad and we'll go meet my squad."

The pigeons and **InvisiFrog** surf through the slimy sewer.

They soon meet four more frogs.

"May I introduce my squad of crime-fighters— the **TRUE FROGS,**" says InvisiFrog.

"This is **Leopard Frog.**

"**Horned Frog.**

"Mmm, flies."

"**Gliding Frog.**

"And **Bullfrog.**"

"This squad looks familiar."

"We live in the sewer because it's peaceful," explains **InvisiFrog.** "Although some evil rats lurk down here. An alligator too!"

"I thought it was just a myth that alligators live in sewers."

"Not rats! They make my feathers freak."

The **UNDERGROUND MONSTER** Homer saw in his vision could have been . . .

a big rat . . .

or an alligator!

"We already know about the stolen water," says **InvisiFrog.** "We're looking into it, aren't we, **TRUE FROGS?**"

"RIBBIT."

"RABBIT."

"ROGER THAT!"

"Do you hear that, **PIGS?**" says Homey. "The frogs are on it. We can return to the **LAND OF SKY!**"

But what if the **UNDERGROUND MONSTER** goes **ABOVEGROUND?** Rock worries it could be the villain that ends the squad.

"We should keep looking for clues aboveground," says Rock. "Just in case—"

"Maybe I'll join you," interrupts **InvisiFrog.** "We can share crime-fighting tips! My squad can keep searching for clues down here."

"RIBBIT." "ROBOT." "ROWBOAT."

So **InvisiFrog** and the pigeons head back up again.

"I've missed you, **LAND OF SKY!**"

Rock is happy to have **InvisiFrog** by their side. And they soon spot trouble.

1. A kitten stuck in a tree.

2. A tree stuck in a kitten.

3. A kitten pretending to be a tree!

Rock needs to save the kitten, the tree, and the birds.

"This is a job for a MASTER OF DISGUISE!" he says.

But **InvisiFrog** leaps forward first.

InvisiFrog saves the kitten stuck in a tree.

Then he saves the tree stuck in a kitten.

Rock can't believe it. InvisiFrog is a MASTER OF DISGUISE too.

There is just the third kitten left.

Rock decides to solve the last problem himself.

"Come here, birdies. I'm just a tree, tee-hee!"

Rock pulls out his tinfoil and dresses up like a fish again.

"Here, kitty kitty!"

He distracts the kitten and saves the birds.

But the kitten pounces.

"Here, fishy fishy!"

"Eeep!"

Feathers go flying. Is the kitten
about to end
the squad...?

InvisiFrog
saves the
day again.

FLING!

PLUCK!

"Lucky I was here, Rock!"
says InvisiFrog.

The **REAL PIGEONS** are bruised and battered. Rock realizes something **TERRIBLE.**

"InvisiFrog is a better **MASTER OF DISGUISE** than me," he says. "My costume only **CAUSED TROUBLE!**"

But **InvisiFrog** and the other pigeons are already off to look for more **MISSING-WATER** clues.

"I know a place we should check!"

Rock doesn't follow.

"If I'm going to protect the squad from ending, I need a better **PIGEON POWER!**" he says.

There's only one thing to do.

He flies back to the empty water fountain.

"Let's hang out with this big flock of pigeons, Trent," he says. "So I can get ideas for a new **PIGEON POWER!**"

But Rock is suddenly just one of many pigeons.

Will he find a new PIGEON POWER?

CHAPTER 3

Someone taps Rock on the shoulder.

"Hello, dear!"

It's one of the other pigeons. "Have you found the water yet?" she asks.

"No." Rock frowns. "The others are on the case. I'm busy looking for a new **PIGEON POWER!"**

"I can help with that, dear," she says. "Barb Pigeon will give that **DROOPY BEAK** a **HAPPY TWEAK!"**

Barb Pigeon shows Rock how to **PECK THE GROUND.**

"If you peck hard enough, you could cause **EARTHQUAKES!"** says Barb.

Then she shows him how to **BOB HIS HEAD.**

"If you bob your head hard enough, you could carve wood like a woodpecker," says Barb.

"Don't watch, Trent!"

Barb Pigeon takes Rock to a power line.

"Or you could try **POOPING WITH PURPOSE,**" she says.

They poop on a car below.

"Hey!"

SPLAT!

SPLAT!

"Maybe pooping will be my new **PIGEON POWER!**" Rock says.

"Barb saves another soul!" says Barb, flying off.

"Rock?" calls a familiar voice.

IT'S TUMBLER!

"Found you."

"Why aren't you with **InvisiFrog** and the others?" Rock says.

"We didn't know where you went," says Tumbler. "So I came to find you. Anyway, **InvisiFrog** is kind of a show-off. He was busy rescuing leaves from a big sewer."

"Isn't it dangerous for us to be so close to this sewer?"

DRAIN TO OCEAN

"I thought we were looking for water and the **UNDERGROUND MONSTER?**"

43

Tumbler squints at Rock strangely. "What are *you* doing?"

Rock blurts out all his feelings at once.

"I'm trying to learn a new **PIGEON POWER** so I can stop whoever is going to end the squad, because I love the **REAL PIGEONS** and I just want to protect us."

Tumbler doesn't seem worried.

In fact, she does a bendy smile.

"Oh, Rock, you are already a **MASTER OF DISGUISE,**"

says Tumbler.

"And you don't have to protect us by yourself. We **ALL** have to protect **EACH OTHER!**"

"But I just learned how to hit a target with my power poops!" says Rock. "Watch this."

He does another poop.

This one shoots into a sewer.

SPLASH-PLOP!

Rock and Tumbler gasp.

"Did that poop just land in . . . water?" cries Rock.

"Sounded like it **SPLASHED BACK!**"

45

"Let's go find that missing water," says Tumbler.

She grabs Rock as she leaps into an open fire hydrant.

"Wait, Tumbler, I'm not bendy like you!"

"Ow!"

BUMP

"Ow!"

THWACK

"Still ow."

STUB

When they come out, they are back in the sewer.

"That's the last time I ever go into a fire hydrant!"

"Oh no!"

Below them is a massive pool. They've found the stolen water.

But it's full of swimming **RATS!**

"InvisiFrog was right," says Rock. "The rats must be the water thieves. Looks like they've made an underground POOL PARADISE!"

Rock and Tumbler lean forward for a better view.

But they get tangled up. *"Uh-oh."*

And fall into the water.

SPLASH!

The pigeons cling to each other as the rats surround them.

The rats are smiling as though they have gotten away with a big crime, like murder or stealing cheese.

The largest rat grabs the pigeons.

"This must be the UNDERGROUND MONSTER!"

"Please don't end our squad!"

The rat hauls them out of the water and . . .

. . . gently dries them off.

"I'm **Rattus** and I'll look after you," says the big rat. "Otherwise, you'll catch a cold."

She wraps the towels around the pigeons. Other rats bring them bread, cheese, and sparkling water.

"What is going on?" says Tumbler.

Rock shakes his head. "Is the rats' evil plan to . . . be nice to us?"

"Of course we're nice!" says **Rattus.** "We're rats!"

"I don't want to be rude," says Tumbler. "But did you steal all this water?"

"No," says **Rattus.** "My RAT PACK and I just stumbled across this place and decided to have a swim."

"We rats live down here to avoid humans," explains **Rattus.** "That's why we're always scurrying away—so we don't scare people!"

InvisiFrog must have been wrong about the rats. They're not evil at all!

"But if you didn't make this **POOL PARADISE,** then who did?" asks Rock. "The alligator?"

"It's just a myth that alligators live in sewers."

Rattus laughs.

At that moment, a scary figure appears, zooming across the water.

"RIDDUP." "GET UP!" "GET OUT!"

"QUICK! SCURRY!"

It's the **TRUE FROGS!**
They hit rats with their tongues.

"They aren't crime-fighters," cries Rock. "They are the **UNDERGROUND MONSTER!**"

53

The rats and pigeons flee.

"The frogs must have been moving stoppers with their tongues," says Rock.

"And diverting pipes," adds Tumbler, "so that water would drain down here to make an **UNDERGROUND POND!**"

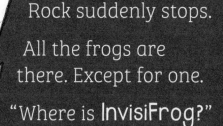

Rock suddenly stops.

All the frogs are there. Except for one.

"Where is **InvisiFrog?**" shouts Rock.

"He probably took us to that big sewer to push us into it," cries Tumbler. "To stop our investigation!"

InvisiFrog must be the one who will end the squad.

ROCK **FLIES** INTO ACTION.

"We have to save our friends!" he says.

CHAPTER 4

Rock and Tumbler exit the sewer. "We need a disguise," says Rock. "Otherwise, **InvisiFrog** will see us coming."

They grab Trent with their feet and spread their wings. Together, they look like a beautiful gray . . .

. . . butterfly!

"We're so pretty!"

They flutter over to the big sewer that leads to the ocean, where they get a shock.

InvisiFrog has tied up Grandpouter, Frillback, and Homey!

DRAIN TO OCEAN

"These ropes are too tight for me to break!"

Frillback yells at **InvisiFrog.**

"Why are you doing this?"

"I can't risk any more of you wandering off." **InvisiFrog** smirks. "You never should have trusted me. You sweet, foolish pigeons!"

InvisiFrog grins. "I'm going to end you pigeons by pushing you down this sewer! Then you won't interrupt our **POND PARADISE** plans."

"But **PIGS** can't **swim!**"

DRAIN TO OCEAN

So **InvisiFrog** is the one who wants to **END** the **REAL PIGEONS!**

"What are we going to do?" wails Tumbler. "If we dive down, **InvisiFrog** will just go invisible and catch us too!"

Rock narrows his eyes. "Invisibility is cool. But I know an even **BETTER** disappearing trick!"

Rock and Tumbler speed back to the water fountain.

"I need your help, Barb Pigeon," says Rock. "In fact, I need **EVERYBODY'S HELP!**"

"Glad you're feeling better, Rock. What can we do?"

Rock explains, and the pigeons all take flight.

The huge flock swoops down, led by Rock, Tumbler, and Barb.

"What above earth is that?"

DRAIN TO OCEAN

The birds land all around Homey, Frillback, and Grandpouter.

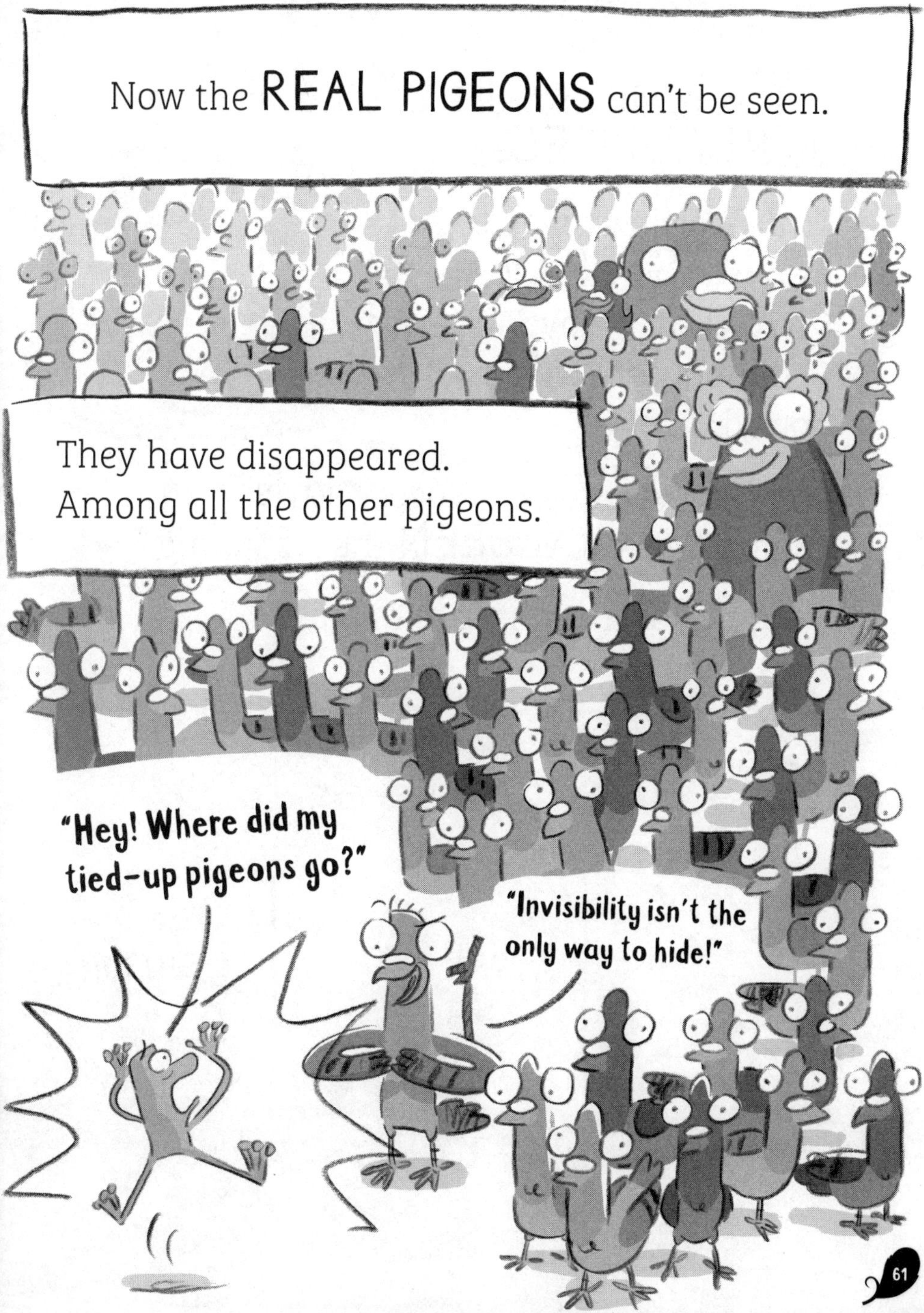
Now the REAL PIGEONS can't be seen.
They have disappeared. Among all the other pigeons.
"Hey! Where did my tied-up pigeons go?"
"Invisibility isn't the only way to hide!"

Hidden by the crowd, Tumbler quickly unties the **REAL PIGEONS.**

"That's a clever way to be a **MASTER OF DISGUISE,**" says Grandpouter. "Well done, Rock!"

"This isn't over, Rock Pigeon!" **InvisiFrog** snarls. "But you've **SEEN** the last of me."

The invisible frog tries to escape.

He leaps into the air . . .

. . . and starts . . .

. . . to fade.

But Rock knows exactly what to do.
He flies up, takes aim, and . . .

POOPS WITH PURPOSE!

InvisiFrog is invisible no more!

"Noooo!"

"Bravo, Rock!"

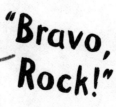

Frillback grabs the floating splatter of poop. "I've got him! Ew."

InvisiFrog turns himself **ON** again with a grumble.

Rattus and her rats appear. They have caught the **TRUE FROGS** with their tails.

"Turns out rat tails are stronger than frog tongues!"

"RIBBIT."

"BUTT IT."

"BLAST IT!"

The rats don't want the frogs living underground anymore.

And the pigeons don't want them aboveground!

So they agree the frogs should be forced to live in between—on the sidewalk.

"Bye, frogs! Watch out for all the human feet!"

"And just when I could use a **POOL** to wash this poop off!"

"We'd better go!" says **Rattus.** "Before we scare any humans."

DRAIN TO OC

Tumbler nudges Rock. "Using pigeons to disguise the squad was genius," she says. "You are the only

MASTER OF DISGUISE who matters."

"Thanks." Rock blushes. "I'm glad I didn't have to protect the squad by myself. You were a big help. So was Barb. And her pigeons. And the rats."

Tumbler and the rats fix the underground pipes.

And everyone returns to the water fountain . . .

... just as it starts raining.

"At least Homer's vision about the squad ending was wrong," says Rock.

"I'm so happy, I don't even need to eat bread crumbs," says Homey. "But I will."

Rock doesn't know what will happen next.

But he knows something for sure.

It will take a lot more than a **vision** and some **bad frogs** to end the REAL PIGEONS squad!

THE END... FOR NOW

LUCKILY...

THE UNDERGROUND POOL
DOESN'T GO TO WASTE.

"A pool?
Just for me?
How wonderful!"

says an alligator.

And the **REAL PIGEONS** keep everyone safe from the big sewer.

"Move on unless you want rainwater to wash you away to the seaside!"

DRAIN TO OCEAN

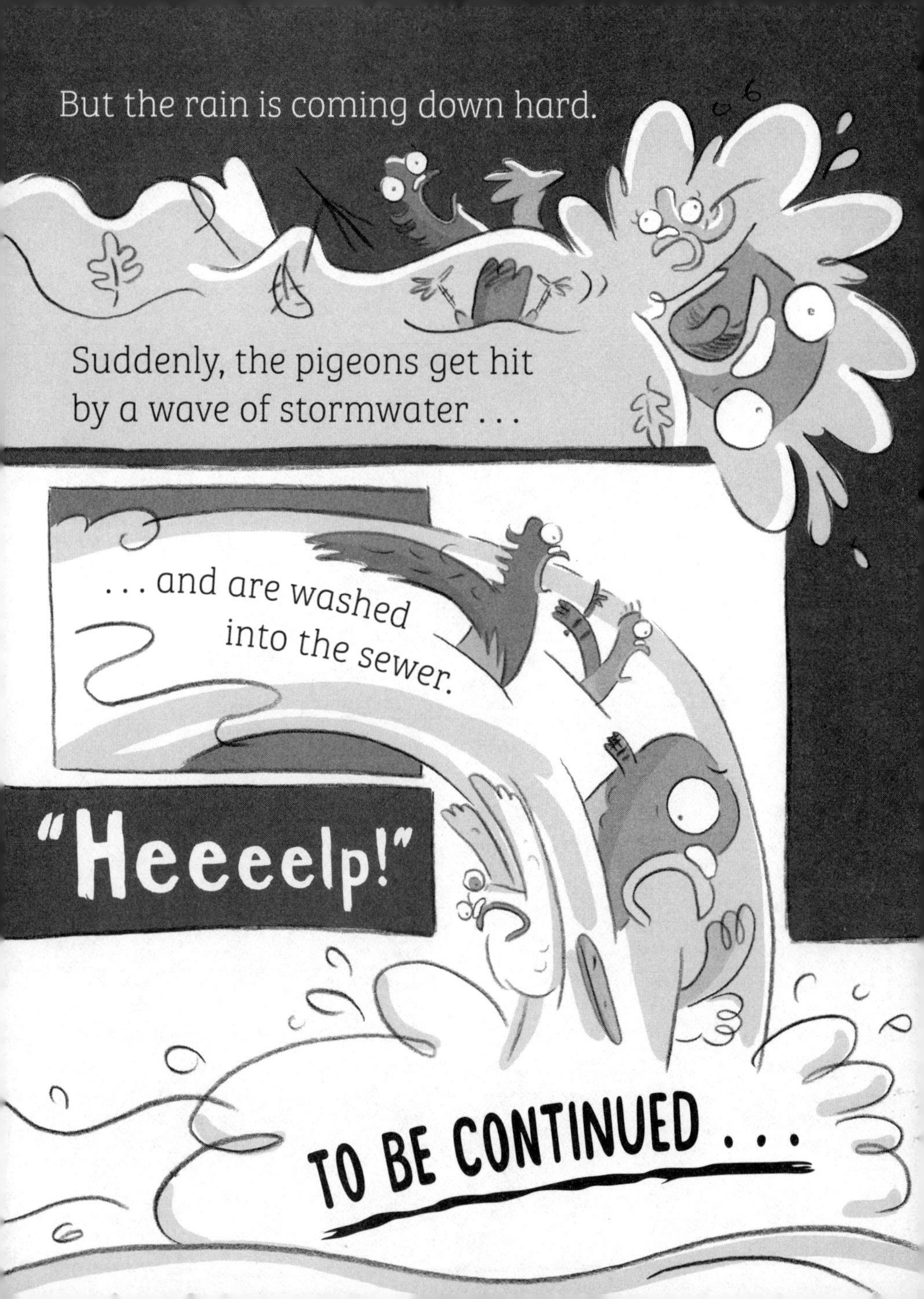

But the rain is coming down hard.
Suddenly, the pigeons get hit by a wave of stormwater . . .
. . . and are washed into the sewer.
"Heeeelp!"
TO BE CONTINUED . . .

PART TWO
SECRETS OF A SEASIDE PRANKSTER

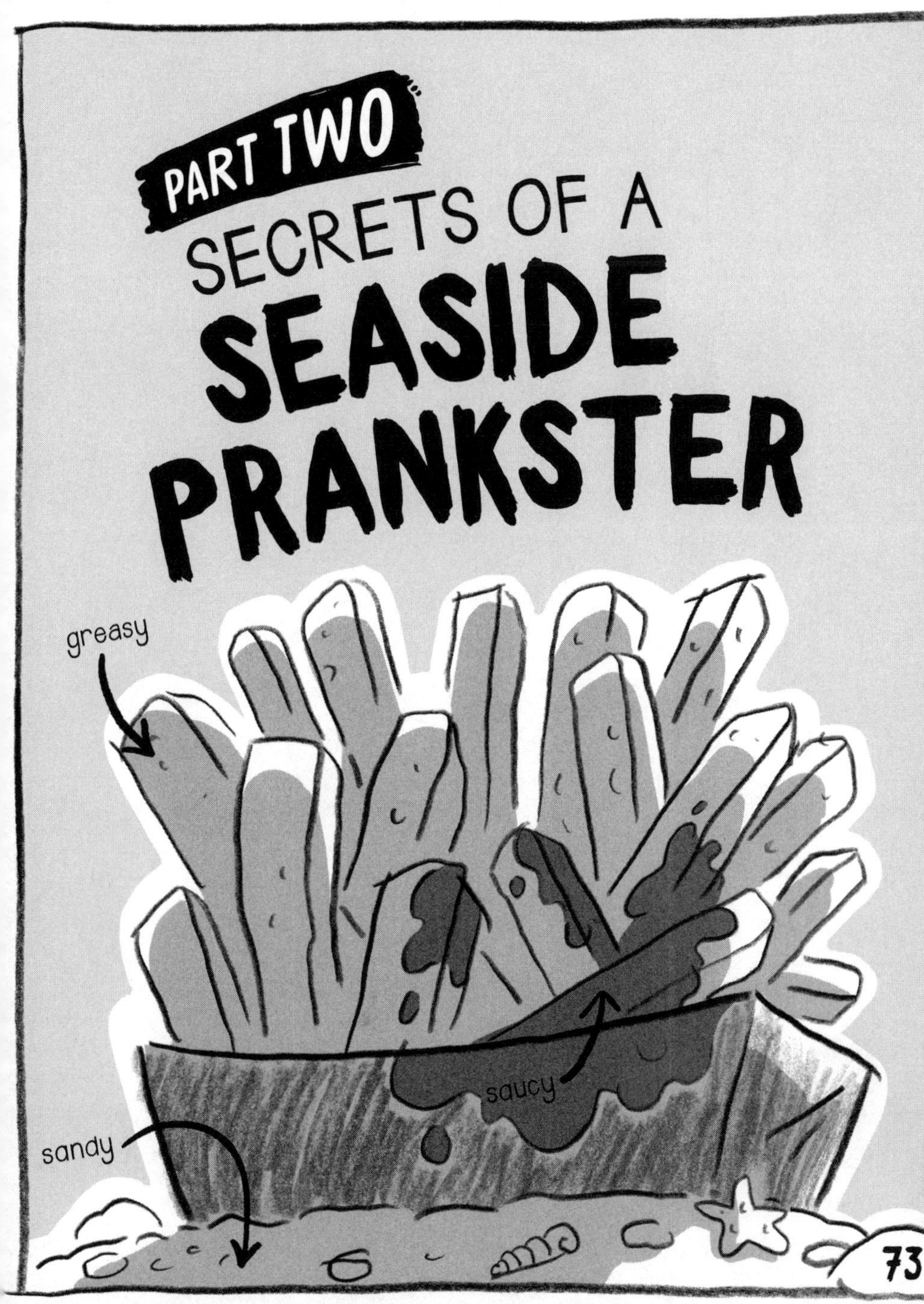
greasy
saucy
sandy

It is a beautiful day at the beach.
The sun is shining.
There isn't a cloud in the sky.
And a pelican is using **seaweed** for fashion.

"This seaweed will make a lovely scarf."

But the peace is about to be broken.

"AHHHHHHHHH!"

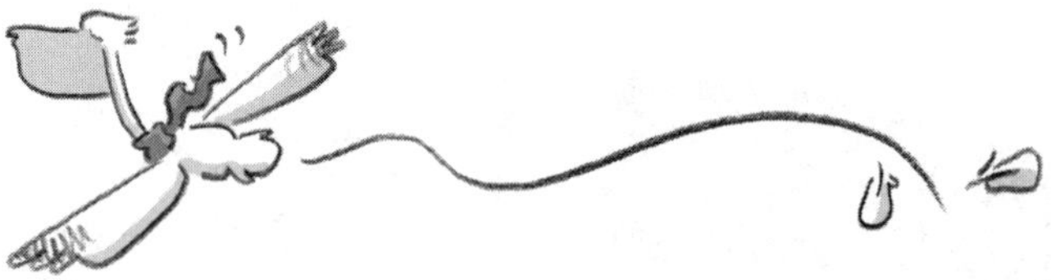

The REAL PIGEONS come rushing out of a drainpipe and land in the ocean.

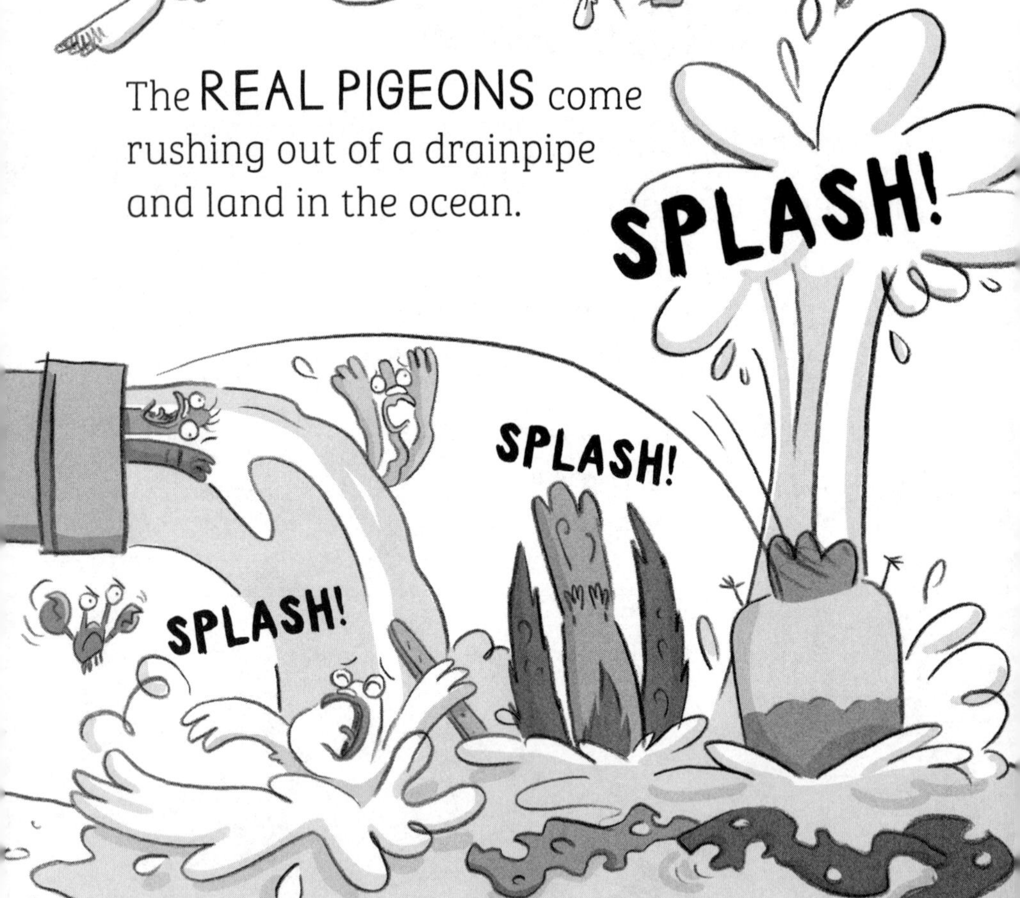
SPLASH!
SPLASH!
SPLASH!

They got swept here from the city during a storm.

Pigeons can't swim. But luckily there is seaweed to grab on to.

They pull themselves onto the sand.

DRIP! DRIP! DRIP!

The water has made Rock's twig, Trent, swell up.

"I can fix anything with my **SUPER STRENGTH**," says Frillback.

She shakes Trent so hard that every last drop flies out of his wooden body.

"We'd better start the long journey back to the city," Rock groans. "Which way, Homey?"

"PIG, we need to eat before we fly!" Homey says. "BITES BEFORE FLIGHTS!"

"But what if we fall in love with the beach before we leave?" cries Rock. "We might quit crime-fighting for a life of leisure."

"Don't worry," says Grandpouter. "We'll have a quick lunch, then head home. The beach won't distract us from ..."

"Did that penguin have ... a beard?" asks Frillback.

The pigeons look around and see more strange things.

Starfish are covered in frosting and sprinkles.

"Are you pretending to be gingerbread?"

"He he!"

A dolphin has a toy cowboy tied to her back.

"LOL!"

And a turtle has googly eyes stuck to his shell.

"Ha ha!"

Humans are laughing, but the **REAL PIGEONS** are confused. Until the angry penguin marches past again.

"There's a **PRANKSTER** in town," he says. "I woke up today and this beard had been drawn on me with a marker!"

The prankster is making beach animals miserable. Rock knows the squad can't leave until . . .

"REAL PIGEONS STOP SEASIDE PRANKSTERS!"

"Hooray!"

The pigeons go looking for the prankster and find they're in a little town at the edge of the beach.

Welcome to
FRY TOWN
POPULATION: 2,984 PEOPLE WHO REALLY LIKE FRIES

The town is called **FRY TOWN** because everyone there is obsessed with . . .

. . . **FRIES!**

FRENCH FRIES

FRENCH FRY FLAVORED **ICE CREAM!**

FRENCH FRY FLAVORED SAUSAGES

"I can't **WAIT** to **EAT** a **FRY TOWN** French fry!" cries Homey.

"Fries are OK, but sausages are better," says Frillback. "They give me my **SUPER STRENGTH!**"

A delivery man rushes past, and Homey catches a loose potato.

"Fries are made from potatoes, which grow underground," Homey explains. "Potatoes are the breads of the earth."

"It **does** look like a lumpy little loaf!"

"Don't forget we're looking for a seaside prankster," says Rock. "That potato is **NOT THE PRANKSTER.**"

not a prankster

A baby throws a French fry to the pigeons. They're about to eat their first **FRY TOWN** fry.

"No, Chester! Feed birds oysters or steak, but never fries!"

"Heads back, beaks open, can't lose!"

But before the French fry reaches the pigeons . . .

. . . a flock of seagulls swoops in and steals it.

Seagulls are jerk birds. Also known as JERDS!

Seagulls are similar to pigeons. With one important difference.

"Those seagulls are so greedy!" cries Rock.

"Time to use my **SUPER STRENGTH** again," says Frillback. "And if you **JERDS** can't share, then no one gets the French fry!"

She grabs the French fry—and the seagulls holding on.

Then throws them far away.

FRY—
SPLASH!

There are just two seagulls left.

Strangely, they appear to be stuck in traffic cones.

The prankster has struck again.

Frillback sets
the seagulls free.

"You got pranked!"
says Rock.
"But at least Frillback didn't
throw you into the—"

One of the seagulls
reaches out and
closes Rock's beak.

"Stop
talking!"

"If we close
your beak, you
will not speak!"

"Yes, we've been pranked,"
says the seagull. "But your
friend Frillback is the real
JERD because she is a
FRENCH FRY WASTER!"

88

"Who are you?" asks Rock.

"I am **Gully,** and this is **Lari,**" says the bird fiercely. "We are seagull wives. Eating fries is hard enough without them being thrown away!"

*"But we won't **despair,** just seek fries **elsewhere!"***

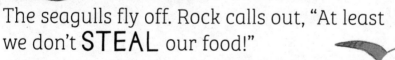

"Lari is a poet!"

The seagulls fly off. Rock calls out, "At least we don't **STEAL** our food!"

"Blah, blah, blah!"

"I can't believe we still haven't eaten a single French fry!" moans Homey.

The pigeons are about to restart the prankster search, when sand flies in their faces.

They close their eyes and hunker down.

"Must be a sandstorm!" cries Rock.

"I hate getting sand in my beautiful feathers, Trent!"

When the sand stops flying, the pigeons are surprised to find they have been **PRANKED.**

frilly hair

Tumbler arm

sandy body

"Hey look, everyone! It's a pigeon mermaid!"

Rock arm

flashy stars

tail

A crowd quickly gathers. People laugh and take photos.

SNAP SNAP **FLASH!**

The pigeons are embarrassed.

"Dress-up isn't fun when it is done TO you!"

"Hey—where did my French fries go?"

And Frillback is horrified. Not because she has sand in her beautiful feathers. But because . . .

"Trent has been **TWIG-NAPPED!**" she cries.

CHAPTER 2

Rock's beak goes limp. "What do you mean Trent has been **TWIG-NAPPED?**"

"I felt someone snatch him from my wing as we were being pranked," moans Frillback.

Gully and Lari fly past and laugh.

"Ha ha—you got **PRANKED** too!"

"It's funny a **smidgen,** since I'm not a **pigeon!**"

A pelican comes along and pulls the pigeons out of the sand.

"Thank you!"

"You're welcome."

Then he shoos away the humans.

"Get out of here, you creatures of skin and hair!"

"I thought you could use a helping wing," he says. "My name is **Paulican.** Did you know the name Paul is short for Paulican?"

Frillback narrows her eyes.

"How did you find us?"

"I have a great view from my lighthouse apartment, and saw that you had been pranked,"

explains Paulican.

"The prankster has stolen Trent—my soulmate and my stickmate!" cries Rock.

Paulican shakes his head. "Dear me," he says. "The prankster is out of control!"

Rock can't help thinking of all the horrible things the prankster might be doing with Trent.

marshmallow stick

dog stick

kebab stick

"Maybe the thief stashed Trent around here?" says Frillback.

"Under this lifeguard?"

"Or under this ice cream truck?"

"Or under this ocean?"

But Frillback can't lift the ocean.

"My **SUPER STRENGTH** should have protected Trent," she says. "I'm so disappointed in you, my muscle!"

Rock and Frillback are miserable.

Tumbler stretches out so she can hug both birds.

"Sorry I'm hugging you with my bottom!"

"Sums up my day!"

"Why would someone steal *my* twig when there are so many free ones lying around?" whimpers Rock.

Frillback suddenly leaps forward and picks up sticks. "Maybe one of these can replace Trent?" she asks.

Frillback gives all the twigs names.

Luna Jethro

Stan

Fernando Lady Byron Agatha

Delilah Lee

Mohammed Tyler Wolf

But there is only
one twig Rock wants.

"I just
want Trent!"

"Then I *will* get Trent back," says Frillback.
"And I'll stop the prankster."

"Nobody knows who the prankster is," says Paulican. "Yet they've pranked almost everyone. The only creatures who have gone **UNPRANKED** are a crab, a ladybug, a stork, a seahorse, and . . . um . . . me."

"I get the feeling he's hiding something, Agatha."

"The prankster has made things personal!" says Grandpouter. "Time for a **SQUAD MEETING.**"

Paulican flies back to his lighthouse. And the pigeons meet on a restaurant chalkboard.

"Today's special is hot French fries stretched out like spaghetti. Covered in a chunky French fry sauce. With grated cheese on top. Except it's not cheese. It's a grated French fry."

FINE DINING

SPAGHETFRY

"The prankster wouldn't prank *themselves*," says Rock. "So it must be one of those **UNPRANKED** animals!"

Tumbler wipes the blackboard clean, twirls herself around a piece of chalk, and draws the five animals.

FINE DINING

SUSPECTS

"One of these animals stole Trent!" says Rock unhappily.

"I'm going to fix everything with my SUPER STRENGTH!"

"We should also help the animals who have already been pranked," says Grandpouter.

He, Homey, and Tumbler find a sandcastle and turn it into a **PRANK HEALING CENTER** . . .

"I'm a barber!"

seaweed flags

"This way for rest and relaxation from pranking."

sand beds

moat

. . . while Rock and Frillback head off to look for the unpranked creatures.

Rock picks up some twigs.

Finds an ice cream cone.

And disguises himself as a stork. Now he can watch to see if the real stork is the prankster.

"Nice day to stalk around as a stork!"

But Rock is so focused on stork-ing that he doesn't notice . . .

... himself getting PRANKED!

It wasn't the stork. But the prankster has sneakily strung up a clothesline between Rock's legs.

FLASH!

FLASH!

SNAP!

"Ha ha!"

CURLY
FRIES

Meanwhile, Frillback spots the ladybug.

SURF SHOP

"Time to use my SUPER STRENGTH!"

She positions herself among some surfboards.

If the ladybug turns out to be the prankster, Frillback will swat him like a mosquito.

But the ladybug accidentally flies into Frillback's beak.

"Sorry about that!"

PLONK!

Frillback coughs and drops the surfboard on herself.

She tries to get up, but . . .

. . . the prankster has sneakily wrapped her up in seaweed.

"Hey, look— a sushi pigeon!"

"Someone stole my fries!"

"Me too! My packet was full a second ago!"

Frillback takes off.

Her **SUPER STRENGTH** hasn't fixed anything yet.

The pigeons meet up again on the restaurant chalkboard.

"The prankster isn't the stork," says Rock. "Or the ladybug," adds Frillback.

Tumbler wipes their pictures off the **SUSPECT BOARD.**

FINE DINING

SUSPECTS

"Why aren't there **FRIES** on the menu??"

"Hmm."

"Hmm."

"Hmm."

Grandpouter frowns. "Then the prankster must be the seahorse, or the crab, or . . ."

"**Paulican!**" says Frillback. "I get the feeling he hasn't told us everything."

FLAP

FLAP

"Whoever the prankster is, we need to be careful," says Rock. "Trent is in danger. And the prankster has been one step ahead of us ever since we arrived at . . . **HEY!**"

FINE D

SUSPEC

The **SUSPECT BOARD** disappears around a distant corner.

"Someone just stole that chalkboard!" cries a waiter.

Rock gulps.

The prankster must have seen the drawings and tried to remove the evidence.

The pigeons are still one step behind. And Trent is still missing!

CHAPTER 3

The **REAL PIGEONS** decide to **QUESTION** the three remaining suspects.

Grandpouter visits the crab but discovers the prankster has already struck. Someone has built a sandy maze around her.

"I just wanted to go out for a crab walk!"

Grandpouter frees the crab. "You are clearly not the prankster," he says.

Homey and Tumbler
visit the seahorse.

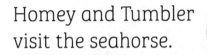

"You're not in any
trouble—just tell us
the truth!"

"But if you don't tell us
the truth, you'll never eat
another bread crumb! Or—
whatever seahorses eat!"

"I'm innocent!" says the seahorse. "Seahorses
can't survive out of water, so I couldn't have
done the pranks on land!"

"Oh yeah! You are clearly
not the prankster."

"OK, bye!"

Rock and Frillback fly up to the lighthouse to question Paulican.

"I'm getting ready to fight the prankster," says Frillback. "I'm still planning on using my **SUPER STRENGTH** to get Trent back."

"Super strength doesn't solve every problem," says Rock.

Fry Town

rocks

lighthouse

They fly through an open window into the lighthouse.

And there is Paulican.

"You won't like this," says Rock. "But we think you might be the prankster."

Paulican doesn't answer. Instead, he gurgles.

GURGLE
GURGLE

"Is everything OK, Paulican?" says Rock.

Paulican sighs and opens his bill.

A fish flaps its fins furiously.

"Help me! I'm too young to fly!"

"What is going on here?" demands Frillback. "Is this another prank?"

"No," says Paulican, gurgling through all the water in his bill. "Let me explain."

"Lighthouses warn ships not to get too close to the rocky land," says Paulican.

"But ships aren't the only things in danger. Ocean creatures sometimes bop their heads on rocks."

BOP!

"Ow!"

"So I live up here, keeping watch. And rescuing animals before they knock themselves out."

"Wait, so you're helping me? Not eating me?"

"That's right. I came up here to look at a map and find out how to take you home!"

"So Paulican isn't the prankster?" says Frillback.

"NO, HE'S A HERO!"
says Rock.

"I have no idea what is going on right now!"

But then Rock sees something. Over the pelican's shoulder. Wedged behind a bookcase.

"Is that ... the **SUSPECT BOARD?!**" cries Rock.

"Oops!"

"You **MUST** be the prankster after all!" yells Frillback.

She jumps on Paulican.
But she jumps too hard.

"Don't spill me!"

They hit the floor,
fall straight through
the floorboards, and . . .

. . . land on something very soft.

"I'm not the prankster!" coughs Paulican. "I stole the blackboard because I didn't want anyone to see it. That is **NOT** a good drawing of me!"

"Oh!" Frillback climbs off him.

"Um, guys," says Rock. "Look at what you're standing on."

The lighthouse is full of . . .

. . . FRENCH FRIES!

Frillback looks at Paulican. "Are these your fries?" she says.

The pelican shakes his head. "I had no idea they were here!"

Rock flies down and picks one up. "I've seen this French fry before," he snorts.

Pigeons have excellent eyesight. And good memories too.

"A human had this French fry at the mermaid prank," says Rock.

Then he recognizes more French fries.

"This French fry was being held by a human at the starfish prank."

"And a human had this French fry at the stork prank."

"The prankster has been stealing fries and stashing them here," says Rock. "But who is it?"

"If only there was a way to return these fries to the people of **FRY TOWN,**" says Paulican.

"There is a way!" Frillback smiles. "Finally I can use my **SUPER STRENGTH** to fix something." She starts stomping her feet.

THUD!
THUD!

THUD!

THUD!

"Wait!"

But it's too late.
Frillback jumps up and down on the fries.

She packs them down and forces them out the lighthouse door.

Where they become one **ENORMOUS** French fry.

But it doesn't stop there.

"Oh no!"

The giant fry slides away down the hill.

Faster and faster.

Straight toward the town below.

FRY TOWN IS ABOUT TO GET MASHED!

The huge French fry hurtles toward **FRY TOWN.**

"I may have made a mistake," says Frillback. "I was so focused on my **SUPER STRENGTH** I forgot our mission. I'm such a **JERD!**"

"You are not a **JERD,**" says Rock. "But you don't always have to use your muscles to fix things."

"Unless a giant French fry is about to destroy the town!" cries Paulican. **"Fix it!"**

Frillback wipes away a tear. "You're right, Paulican. I have to make this right."

She launches after the giant fry.

But it's moving faster than a rocket.

"It's a FRY-MERGENCY!"

"Not again!"

Frillback zooms in front of the fry. She uses every muscle in her body to try to stop it.

The giant fry slows but still slides into town.

Where it crushes a French fry stand.

And is about to run over
some twigs . . .

"Run, Fernando,
Agatha, and Stan!"

. . . when it stops.

"Phew."

"Hi, PIGS."

127

FRY TOWN is saved! And there is suddenly a big feast in the middle of town.

"Time to eat the Godzilla French fry!"

"Best day ever!"

Homey and the pigeons finally get to eat some fries.

The seagulls are overjoyed too.

Or—most of them are.

Gully and Lari
are crying.

"This is terrible!" wails Gully. "Everyone is eating the fries we spent months stealing!"

"We've caught our pranksters," says Frillback, crossing her big wings. "I think Gully and Lari pretended to be pranked so we wouldn't suspect them."

"Being **caught** is a very bad **thought!**"

"But why did you need **SO MANY** fries?"

"Fine, yes, we're the pranksters," admits Gully. "Doing pranks is the only way we can steal fries from humans without fighting other seagulls, and—"

Rock reaches out and closes Gully's beak.

"You are greedy **JERDS**," he says. "Now where is Trent?"

"You have no idea what you're talking about!" says Gully. She hauls Rock into the air. "I'll show you!"

"Hey!"

131

The birds follow Gully and Rock.

They land on a roof
with many chimneys.

"We were doing pranks to
steal fries!" says Gully. "But
not because we're greedy.
The fries were for **Gully Junior.**"

"Who?"

The pigeons peer inside an unused chimney and see a tiny seagull chick.

"Fries are hard to come by for birds in **FRY TOWN,**" says Gully. "So we were collecting a lifetime supply for our baby."

"I'm sorry," says Rock. "You're not **JERDS**—you're loving parents!"

But then he notices something.

"Is your chick cuddling... **TRENT?**"

"I took that twig because I thought Gully Junior would like it," admits Gully. "Don't you dare try to take it away from her!"

"I will fix this," says Frillback, stepping forward. Rock thinks she's about to use her **SUPER STRENGTH** again.

But instead she holds out her wing. "Let's make a deal. If you give Trent back, I'll show you how to make your own **FRENCH FRIES!**"

"I'm a reasonable gull," says Gully.

"Deal!"

The pigeon and the seagull smoosh their wings together (which is the bird version of a handshake).

Rock winks at Frillback. "Nice!"

Frillback finds some potatoes.

Cuts them up with her talons.

And bakes them on a chimney.

"Brilliant idea, Frillback!"

"Thanks for the tip—now who wants a French fry?"

"And here's something for you, Rock!"

Rock and his stickmate are reunited.

And the pigeons and seagulls share a dinner of home-cooked FRIES!

"Eating is another thing I can do without my SUPER STRENGTH!"

THE END

THE GOOD NEWS IS . . .

PAULICAN AND THE FISH BECOME FAST FRIENDS.

They team up to become a **ROCK RESCUE** and save sea creatures from bopping their heads on rocks.

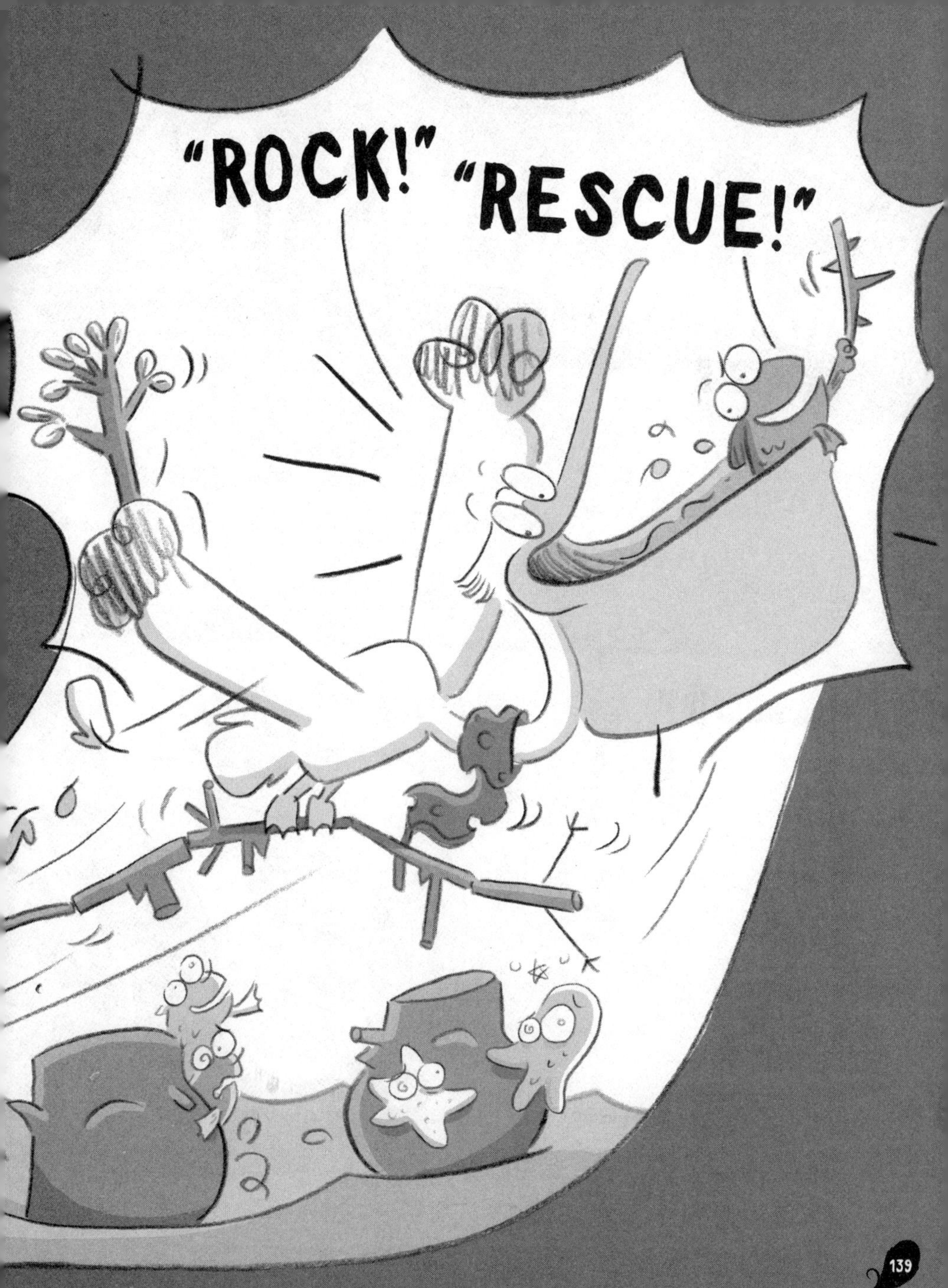
"ROCK!"
"RESCUE!"

THE BAD NEWS IS ...

AS THE PIGEONS FLY HOME, FRILLBACK GETS SICK.

"This way, PIGS!"

"I don't feel well. Can pigeons get travel sickness?"

The squad finally arrives home.
But Frillback is clearly not well.
"I don't think you're TRAVEL SICK,"
says Rock worriedly.
"I think you're SICK SICK!"
"We need to get her some help!"
TO BE CONTINUED . . .

PART THREE THE POLKA-DOT CRISIS

Rock Pigeon loves shoeboxes.

They are good for keeping costumes in.

And for spying in.

And for playing robots in.

"Coo-operate or be exterminated!"

MAIL

But shoeboxes are most useful when . . .

. . . a bird gets sick.

Frillback has a bad cough and is covered in spots. So Rock has found her a shoebox to rest in.

Shoeboxes are the hospital beds of the pigeon world.

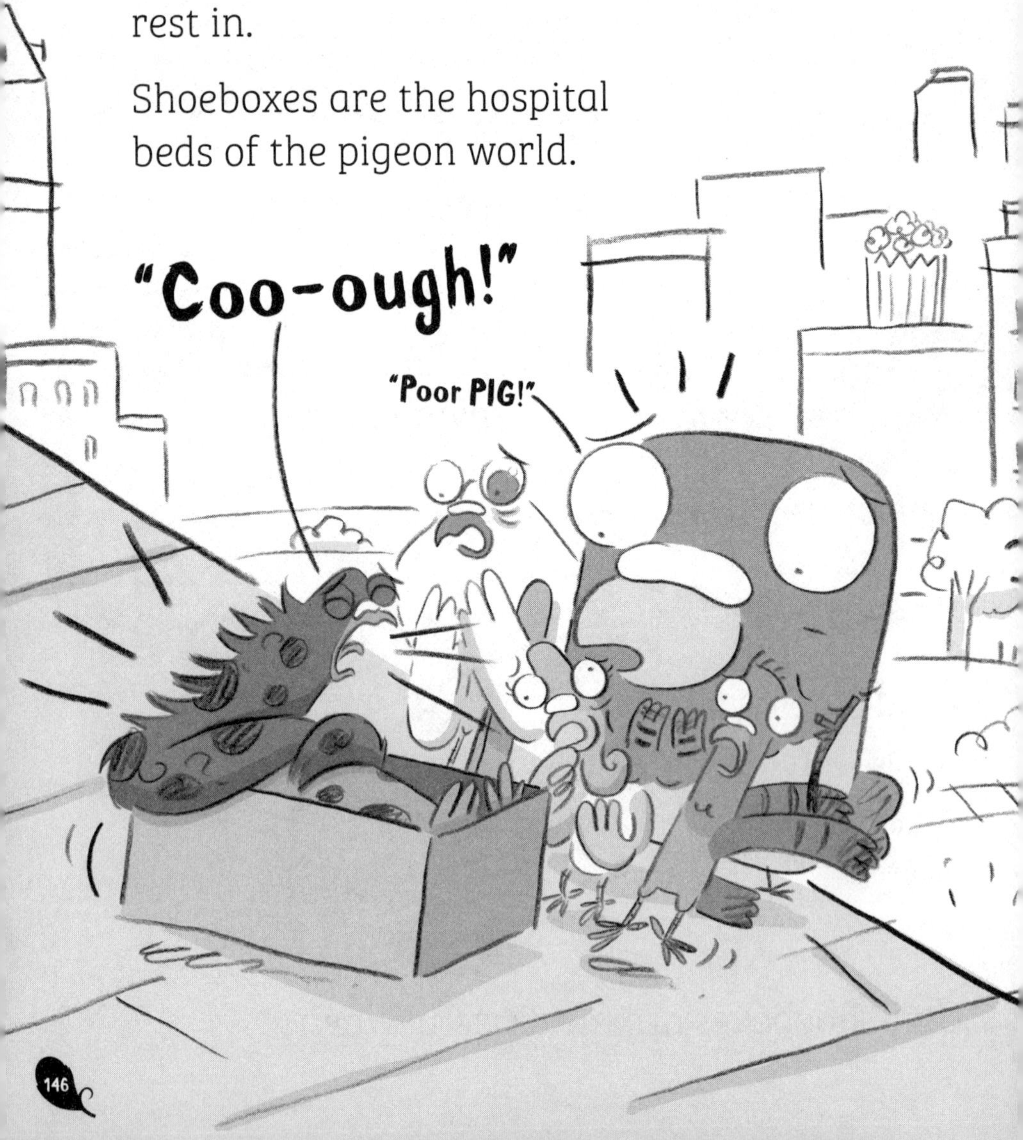
"Coo-ough!"
"Poor PIG!"

The pigeons are on the roof of their gazebo. They are trying to comfort Frillback.

Homey gives her a teddy-bear cookie.

Grandpouter gives her a stamp.

"It's art for the wall of your shoebox!"

And Tumbler gives her a sausage.

But Frillback doesn't eat the sausage.

Or **hug** the teddy bear.

Or admire the stamp.

She is **REALLY** sick. Rock hopes the sickness doesn't spread. The squad won't be able to fight crime if they're **ALL** in shoeboxes.

So Rock goes flying. And spots a toy soldier with a parachute, left in a playground sandpit.

He takes it to Frillback and ties it on like a medical mask.

"You won't spread dot-germs now!"

"We need to look after Frillback," Grandpouter says. "But we also have to protect the city. I heard crime increased while we were at the beach."

Tumbler and Homey stay to care for Frillback while Rock and Grandpouter leave to **FIGHT CRIME.**

Out in the park they run into a flock of pigeons, led by Barb Pigeon. Rock tells her about Frillback.

"Your friend isn't the only sick pigeon around here, dear," says Barb, looking worried.

"There's a sick pigeon resting under a park bench."

"And another one on top of a vending machine."

BEAR LEMONADE: FIZZY AND FUZZY!

"And another in a shoe shop."

"Hey! This isn't a pair of size 10 iguana-green sneakers!"

The mystery pigeon sickness is spreading!

"I'm distributing shoeboxes to all the sick pigeons, poor darlings," says Barb.

Rock is starting to get **VERY** concerned. But then he notices something else.

BIG, BRIGHT POLKA DOTS HAVE APPEARED IN THE PARK!

"Have these polka dots always been here?"

he asks.

"They aren't just dots!" says Grandpouter. "They are **GRAFFITI,** and that is a **CRIME!**"

"Look, there's more!" says Rock.

The pigeons investigate.

The polka dots are everywhere. They are causing **TROUBLE** at traffic lights.

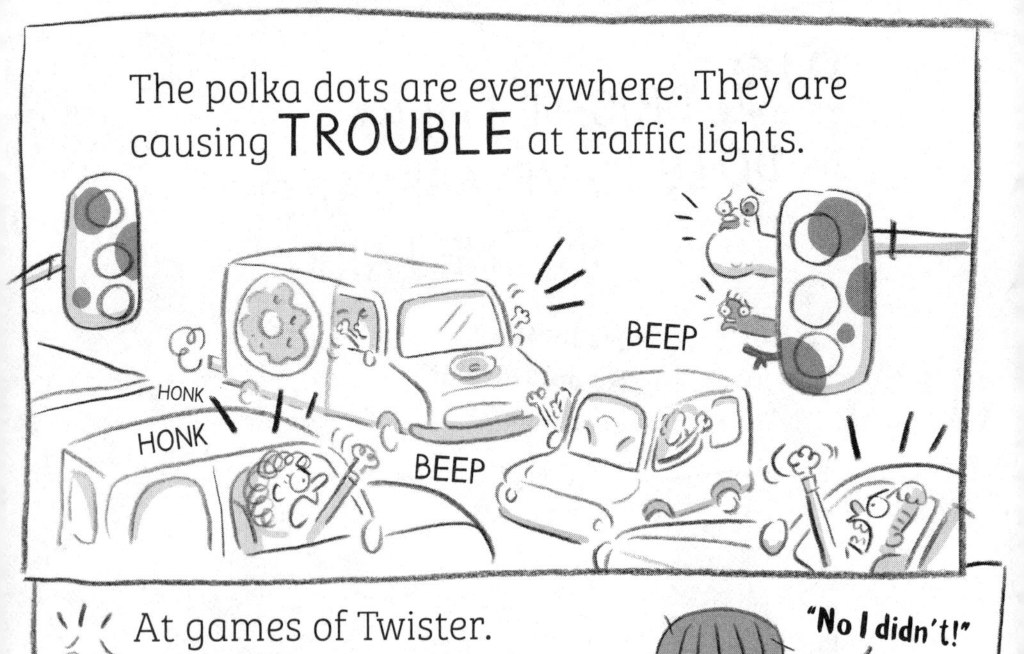
BEEP
HONK
HONK
BEEP

At games of Twister.

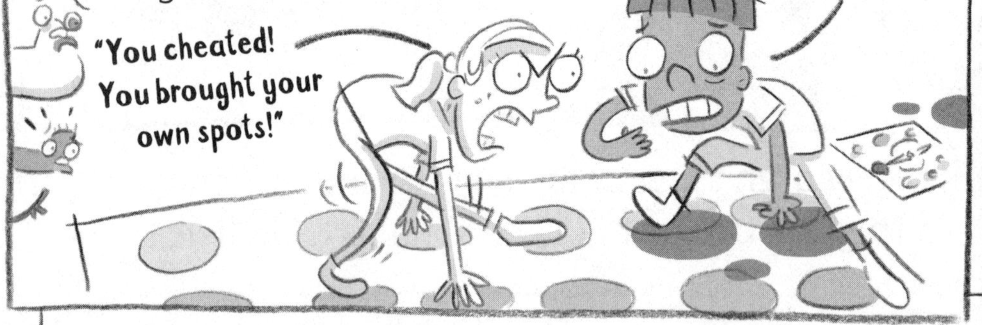
"No I didn't!"
"You cheated! You brought your own spots!"

And near important signs.

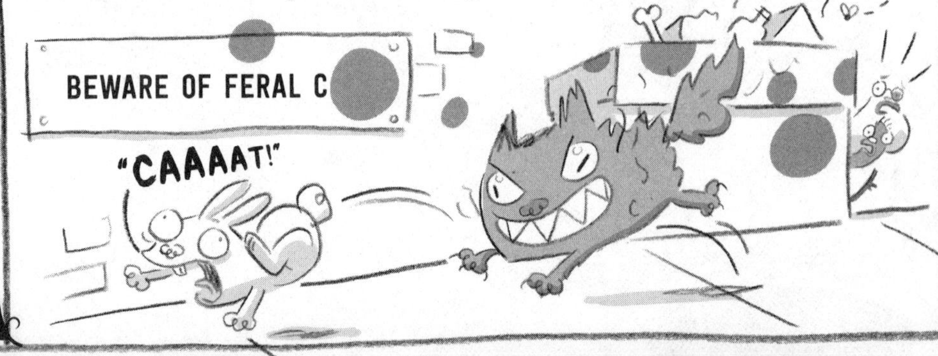
BEWARE OF FERAL C
"CAAAAT!"

"SO DO YOU LIKE MY POLKA DOTS— OR WHAT?"

cries a voice.

Rock and Grandpouter spin around.

Against a wall they see the shadow of a giant, hideous **spider thing.**

"Who are you?"
cries Rock.

"YOU CAN CALL ME CYCLON— BECAUSE THAT IS MY NAME!"

the creature spits.

155

"I LOVE POLKA DOTS!"

hollers **Cyclon.** "So I'm painting the city spotty!"

"Graffiti is a **CRIME!**" says Rock. "And we are crime-fighters. When our friend Frillback is better, she'll toss you far away into the sky!"

"OH NO SHE WON'T!" **Cyclon** laughs. "Because I'm the one who made her sick with dots, and I'm the only one who can make her better!"

Rock is shocked. "You **DOT-GERMED** Frillback?"

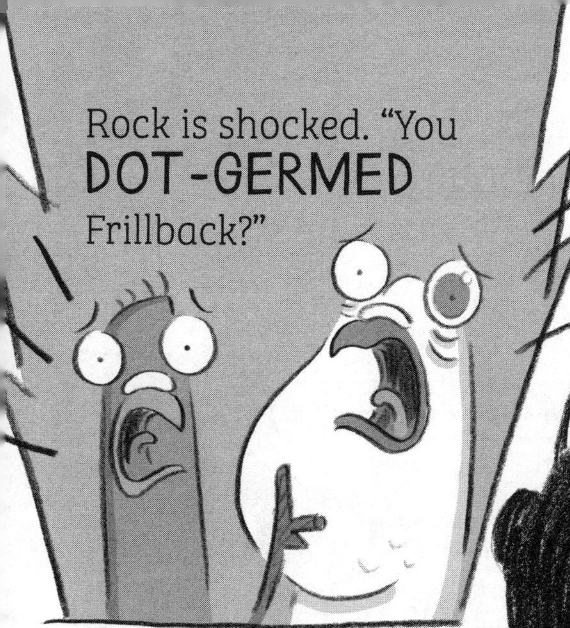

"I SURE DID!" Cyclon sneers. "I'm dot-germing everyone—because I want the whole city to go dotty!"

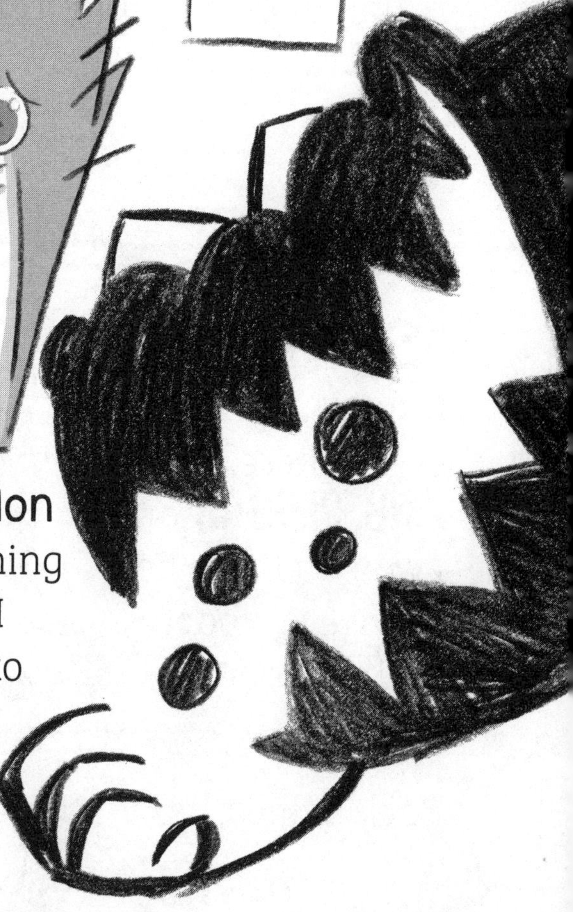

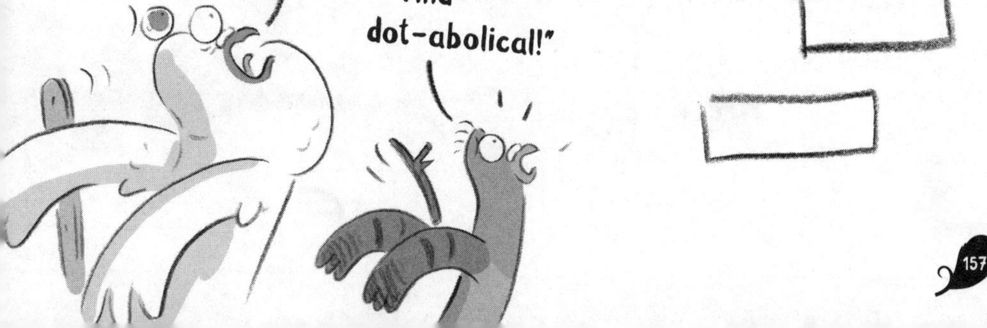
"That's diabolical!"
"And dot-abolical!"

"Reveal yourself!" Rock cries, running toward **Cyclon's** shadow. "I want to see who you are!"

"**STOP!**" booms **Cyclon,** spraying spit everywhere. "**COME ANY CLOSER** and I won't tell you how to save Frillback and the others!"

Rock halts.

"There's no need to spit!"

says Grandpouter.

"What if a pigeon accidentally slips on it?"

"How do we cure Frillback, then?" asks Rock nervously.

"WORK FOR ME," says Cyclon.
"Give up fighting crime and paint polka dots everywhere instead!"

"Never!" shouts Rock.
"We're not criminals!"

"If you don't, **I'LL KEEP SPREADING DOT-GERMS!**" says Cyclon.
"I lurk everywhere and no one notices! You have one hour to decide. But right now I need to go pee. I had a big drink right before this conversation!"

Without another word, **Cyclon** and his shadow are gone.

"Where'd he go?"

"I'm guessing to pee?"

Rock and Grandpouter frown at each other.

"There's got to be another way to stop the germs!" says Grandpouter. "Because the **REAL PIGEONS** could never be **REAL CRIMINALS.**"

Could they?

CHAPTER 2

Rock and Grandpouter return to the gazebo.

Frillback is still very unwell.

"We got rid of her mask after she threw up a little."

Rock tells the others about **Cyclon.** "I have no idea who he really is," he says. "He looks like a big spider. Or a chewed-up tennis ball! Or an apple eaten by a zigzaggy caterpillar."

"He doesn't sound very scary to me!"

The pigeons agree not to become polka-dot criminals. Instead, they vow to track down **Cyclon** and get the cure themselves.

"REAL PIGEONS STOP DOTS!"

Rock is wondering **HOW** they will find **Cyclon,** when Homer swoops down.

"Rock," he wheezes.
"We need to talk!"

HOMER
(Homey's dad,
gets visions, has
fluffy beard)

"I've had another vision about the REAL PIGEONS squad ending," says Homer.

"Didn't we already stop InvisiFrog and those frogs from ending the squad?" asks Rock.

"The squad is **still** going to end," sighs Homer. "And my latest vision showed that YOU will end it, Rock!"

"Me?"

Rock is shocked.

And he does something unexpected.

He bursts into laughter.

"HA! HA! HA! HA! HA! HA!"

"Homer, that is such a RELIEF!" Rock giggles. "There's NO WAY *I'm* going to end the squad. I'm not a BAD BIRD! So your VISION must be wrong!"

"I've never had a vision that didn't come true," says Homer. **"But we'll find out soon enough, PIGLET!"**

Before Rock can reply, he hears a big . . .

"Coo-ough!"

Frillback is looking sicker and sicker. They need to find **Cyclon** and that cure, **FAST!**

"Let's start our search in the park," suggests Rock.

At that, Frillback smiles weakly. So the pigeons turn her shoebox into a stroller.

bread-roll wheels

As they walk through the park, they discover that **cyclon** has dot-germed other animals too.

"I'm not a dalmation— just a dog covered in spots!"

"I'm not a leopard— just a cat covered in spots!"

"I'm not a giraffe— just an alpaca covered in spots!"

"No one thought you were a giraffe, **DUDE!**"

"Why is there even an alpaca at the park?"

Then they see **Rattus,** who usually sticks to the sewers.

"Don't look down, humans. Rats are lovely, but you'll freak out!"

"I heard Frillback was sick, so I got her a get-well cheese," says **Rattus.** "But someone painted it with dots when I wasn't looking!"

"Cyclon strikes again," says Rock.

"I might as well eat it," says **Rattus,** gobbling the cheese. "Hey, polka dots taste delicious!"

She bounds away, and Rock wonders if **Rattus** is **Cyclon.** She ate dots and doesn't seem worried about getting dot-germed.

The pigeons soon discover that their gazebo has been painted in dots too. The entire city is going dotty!

Cyclon is OUT OF CONTROL.

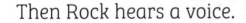

Then Rock hears a voice.

"PIDGIES!"

It’s one of their favorite neighborhood kids!

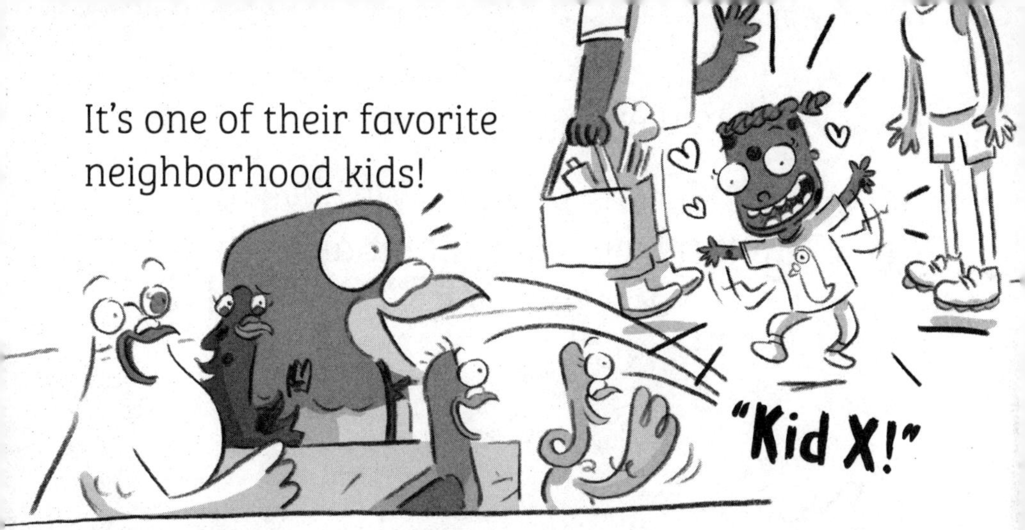
"Kid X!"

“PIDGIES!” cries the kid. “I sick with spots!”

The pigeons hug the kid.

"I have no idea how she got sick! I never let her out of my sight!"

Rock knows what happened. **Cyclon** has dot-germed her too. This is really bad. If humans all get sick, that means NO BREAD CRUMBS for anyone!

Rock has had enough.

"This can't go on," he says. "We have to stop **Cyclon** from using paint and germs to put polka dots on EVERYONE AND EVERYTHING!"

"It's time we had an EMERGENCY MEETING," says Grandpouter.

"**Cyclon** could be lurking anywhere, so we need to go somewhere private!" declares Rock.

170

They can't push Frillback in the stroller anymore because Homey has eaten the wheels.

"I had to! They were getting dirty!" Homey cries.

"Let's take our

NEST PLANE,"

says Tumbler.

NEST PLANE

The pigeons bundle into their nest and fly off.

They have their meeting above the city.

And Rock says something shocking.

"The germs are spreading too quickly, so I think we should do what **Cyclon** suggested," says Rock.

"We should become POLKA-DOT CRIMINALS!"

"**What?**" "Gasp!"

"Coo-ough!"

Is Rock trying to **END** the squad?!

He explains his idea.

Just as they pass a factory wall, someone shouts, **"HEY, PIGEONS!"**

It's **Cyclon!**

"He's way scarier than a spider, an apple, or a tennis ball!"

"YOUR HOUR IS UP!" he slobbers.

"Are you ready to turn criminal and paint the town spotty? I'm tired of doing all the work."

"**OK,**" says Rock fiercely. "We will be polka-dot criminals for you. But you have to promise to cure everyone and stop spreading germs!"

"OF COURSE!" says **Cyclon.** "Once I see you painting polka dots everywhere, I will give you the cure!"

Grandpouter leans over the edge of the **NEST PLANE.** "Why don't you show yourself?"

"You already know me!" **Cyclon** snarls. "Now get polka-dotting, pigeons. And **NO FIGHTING CRIME!** Or else the deal is off!"

Cyclon vanishes, and the pigeons land on the street.

"Time for us to get **CRIMINAL!**" Rock grins.

He digs through a garbage can and picks out a pair of leather gloves, some crayons, and some safety pins.

The **REAL PIGEONS** cut and stitch and draw until they look . . .

The **REAL PIGEONS** look around to make sure **Cyclon** isn't nearby.

Then they whisper,

"REAL PIGEONS GO UNDERCOVER!"

CHAPTER 3

The **REAL PIGEONS** have a plan. They just have to get close enough to **Cyclon** to catch him.

But first, they must convince him that they're criminals. So they paint polka dots on a wall.

"The smaller the dots, the smaller the crime—right?"

ketchup dots →

"I wonder why **Cyclon** always keeps to the shadows," Rock whispers. "What's he hiding?"

"**Cyclon** said we know him, so maybe he's someone in disguise," replies Grandpouter. "Like the frogs. Or the seagulls? Or . . ."

"**HELLO!**"

It's **Rattus.** She is holding a box of chocolates.

"Since my cheese didn't work out, I've brought chocolates for Frillback." She grins. "I nibbled **F**s on them! What are you doing?"

Rock doesn't know if **Rattus** is **Cyclon.** Or if **Cyclon** is secretly watching. So he stays UNDERCOVER.

"We're not crime-fighters anymore," he says rudely. "We're criminals!"

"Yeah!" says Tumbler. "We're so bad we fly into windows just to scare humans!"

"I call it THE WINDOW PAIN!"

"That's disappointing," says **Rattus.** "I never thought you'd end up in the gutter."

"The gutter?" repeats Rock.

"Yes, that gutter over there," says **Rattus.** "That's where **BAD BIRDS** and other criminals hang out."

Rock and the squad see the gutter is full of creatures making plans to do **CRIME.**

There are even some familiar faces.

"I'm going to pinch gold foil from a craft shop! I'll be rich in very thin gold!"

GOLDPINCH (bad finch who likes gold a lot)

"I'm going to steal myself a flashy new shell!"

snail who can't resist temptation

"There is more crime going on in the city than I realized!" Rock shivers.

Rock watches helplessly as different criminals head off. The **REAL PIGEONS** could never fight all this crime at once.

But right now they need to catch **Cyclon.** So Tumbler approaches the **TRUE FROGS.**

"I'll give you a **golden lily pad** if you can help me find a villain named Cyclon!"

Luckily, the frogs don't recognize Tumbler in her disguise.

"Today's your lucky day, **BAD BIRD!**" says **InvisiFrog.** "We'll take you to him."

The frogs take the pigeons to the darkest corner of the garden.

"This is where **Cyclon** lives," says **InvisiFrog.**

There, they discover **Cyclon's** giant, menacing shadow on the wall.

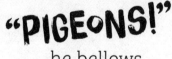 **"PIGEONS!"** he bellows. "How did you find me? And what is so urgent? Haven't you heard of text or email?"

183

The pigeons stay still.

They are frozen.
They do not
answer.

"Why do you not
speak, pigeons?
Do I scare— **HEY!**"

There is a clatter, and
Cyclon's shadow
suddenly disappears.
Because these are
not pigeons.

They are actually . . .

. . . the **TRUE FROGS!**

"When is that **BAD BIRD** coming back with the golden lily pad?!"

"The frogs reminded me of . . . us!"

Meanwhile, the **REAL PIGEONS** have crept up on **Cyclon** and backed him into a corner.

They are amazed to discover he is . . .

. . . a ladybug!

"You're tiny!" gasps Rock, grabbing the flashlight. "How have you been dot-germing animals?"

"EASY!" cries **Cyclon.** "I fly into mouths and dribble! Ladybugs have special germs, and my spit causes sickness and spots!"

"Sorry about that! (He he!)"

"Why did you disguise yourself as a giant shadow?" asks Rock.

Cyclon laughs wildly. "No one ever suspects ladybugs of crime! I didn't want to ruin our reputation. But when I'm just a shadowy monster, I can be my **TRUE SELF!**

HA HA HA!"

Rock shudders.

Even though **Cyclon** is small, he can make anyone sick! He might be the most dangerous creature Rock has ever met.

Cyclon flutters his wings creepily. "You're obviously still fighting crime, so our deal is off. Now I'm going to make the entire city sick. By pouring this bottle of **LADYBUG SPIT** into a water tower! Everyone will soon be covered in **POLKA DOTS**—just like Frillback and the others!"

"No!" cries Rock.

"It took me a long time to save this much spit," Cyclon adds. "I spat into this bottle every day for a year."

The pigeons dive at the evil ladybug.

But **Cyclon** is too small and swift.

He zigzags through the air and slips through their feathers.

Then he's gone. The **REAL PIGEONS** have lost a dangerous criminal. And there's still no cure for Frillback.

"How are we going to guard **ALL** the water towers in the city?" cries Tumbler.

As they speed back to the gazebo, Rock sees something incredible.

LOTS OF FLOCKS OF
PIGEONS!

The **REAL PIGEONS** swoop down,
amazed to see so many birds in one place.

Barb Pigeon and **Rattus**
are here too.

"Rock! So glad
to see you, dear!"

"Does this mean you
aren't criminals anymore?"

"Why are you all gathered on this rooftop?"
asks Rock.

"I've brought all the healthy pigeons here so they don't catch the spotty germs!" says Barb.

"We love Barb!" chant the pigeons.

"We had a feeling you were just working **UNDERCOVER,**" **Rattus** giggles. "So we've been fighting crime for you in the meantime."

"You have?"

"I caught a bird called Goldpinch who was stealing gold foil," says Barb. "I used my **POOPING PIGEON POWER!**"

"And even though I'm a rat, I used the **PIGEON POWER** of flight!" cries **Rattus.** "I caught a snail stealing a fancy shell."

Rock is amazed and proud.

But he's also feeling sad. Because the **REAL PIGEONS** have failed. They couldn't even catch a ladybug. Barb and **Rattus** had to be heroes. And the city is dotty and full of crime.

Rock thinks hard. Maybe the squad should consider its future?

He talks to the squad. And they agree. Something needs to change.

Rock flies onto a crate.

"Hello, everyone," he cries. "I am Rock, a member of the **REAL PIGEONS** squad. And I have an announcement. As of this moment I am **ENDING** the **REAL PIGEONS** squad. For good!"

"What?"

"Huh?"

"No!"

A clever smile blooms on Rock's beak.

"That's right," he says. "There is too much crime in the city for us to handle alone. So we're ending the **REAL PIGEONS** squad. And starting something new called . . .

THE REAL PIGEONS WORLD WILD NETWORK!"

"And the best part is that ANY pigeon can join!" cries Rock.

"So who is with us?" asks Grandpouter.

At first the crowd is silent.
But then Barb speaks up. "I'll join you!"

More and more pigeons
add their voices.

"Me coo!"
"Me coo!"
"Me coo!"
"Me coo!"
"Me coo!"
"Me coo!"
"Me coo!"
"Me coo!"
"Me coo!"
"Me coo!"
"Me coo!"
"Me coo!"

Every single pigeon there wants to fight crime.

"Can I join too?" asks **Rattus**. "I'm not a pigeon. But I can fly now!"

"Why not?" Rock grins. "We have our first case! We need to stop **Cyclon** the ladybug from germing the city's water supply."

REAL PIGEONS STOP EVIL LADYBUGS!

"I thought Rock ending the squad would be a **BAD THING,**" says Homer, wiping away a tear. "But this is **AMAZING.** And my vision was right after all!"

"Now listen up," says Rock. "This is how we're going to catch **Cyclon!**"

The pigeons of the **REAL PIGEONS WORLD WILD NETWORK** fly across the city sky.

They stop for a quick drink and a splash at the water fountain.

GULP
GULP
GULP!

After all, they are still pigeons.

Then they fly up and surround each of the city's water towers, protecting them from **Cyclon.**

Meanwhile, Rock and the gang watch and wait until they see . . .

. . . the signal!

Some of the pigeons
are in arrow formation.

"Those pigeons have
found **Cyclon!**" cries Rock.

All the pigeons
swoop down.

And there is **Cyclon.**

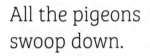

SLOSH

"GRRR!"

But even though he is surrounded, no one can actually grab him.

Cyclon is still too small, too fast, too nimble.

"Time to splash my germs through the city!" He sneers.

"That's not going to happen." Rock grins. "Because there's something you don't know."

"What's that?" Cyclon laughs.

"REAL PIGEONS SPLASH BACK!"

cries Rock.

The pigeons open their beaks. Water comes pouring out. And Cyclon is drenched.

The **REAL PIGEONS** network is already a crime-fighting success!

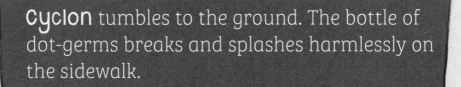

Cyclon tumbles to the ground. The bottle of dot-germs breaks and splashes harmlessly on the sidewalk.

And two wings clap around the evil ladybug.

CLAP!

"Guess what," says Frillback. "I'm feeling better."

"YEAH," Cyclon sighs. "You don't really need a cure for my germs. They just wear off."

"What?!" Rock cries. Then he looks closely at Cyclon. "Hang on, your dots are coming off!"

For the first time, **Cyclon** doesn't look evil at all. He looks defeated.

"I'm a ladybug without dots." He sighs. "But **IT'S NOT FAIR.** I love dots. So I've been covering the world in polka dots to make up for it and—"

Cyclon doesn't say another word.

Because Frillback has dropped him into a jar.

"I'm going to keep **Cyclon,**" says Frillback. "He can be my **ENEMY PET.** Like when humans own snakes."

From the top of the water tower, Rock watches the birds flying away.

They are all pigeons.

And all crime-fighters!

"Crime-fighting is great, but now it's dinnertime."

"Enjoy! You've earned it."

The REAL PIGEONS WORLD WILD NETWORK is going to be AWESOME!

The **REAL PIGEONS**, Barb, and **Rattus** all fly back to the gazebo.

"We've got some work to do," says Rock. "To figure out how to run this network."

A new pigeon era has truly begun.

209

And far away, out at sea, two pigeons fly together.

"Have you heard that pigeons everywhere are coming together to join a crime-fighting network?"

"I've always wanted to fight crime!"

"Time to spread the **GOOD COOS** to the rest of the world!"

THE END

UNFORTUNATELY...

THERE IS SOMETHING THE REAL PIGEONS DON'T KNOW.

Barb Pigeon is about to join the meeting.

When she stops.

And takes off her head.

Barb Pigeon is actually . . .

. . . JUNGLE CROW!

The REAL PIGEONS' number one enemy!

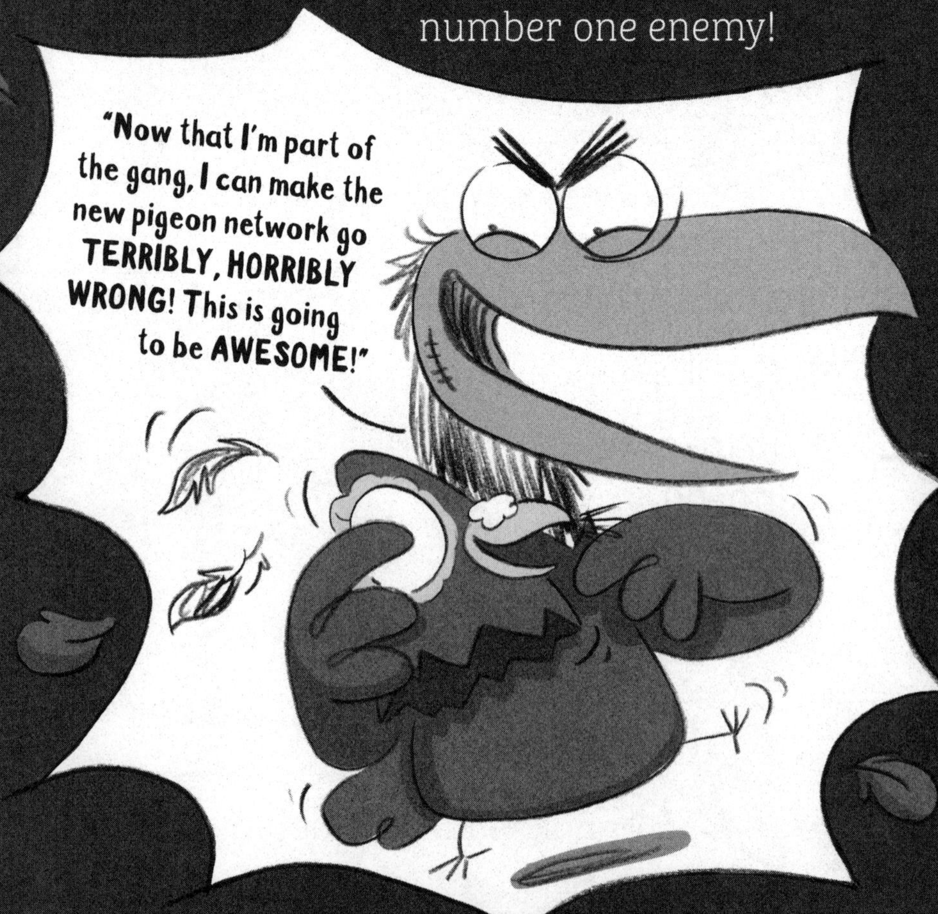

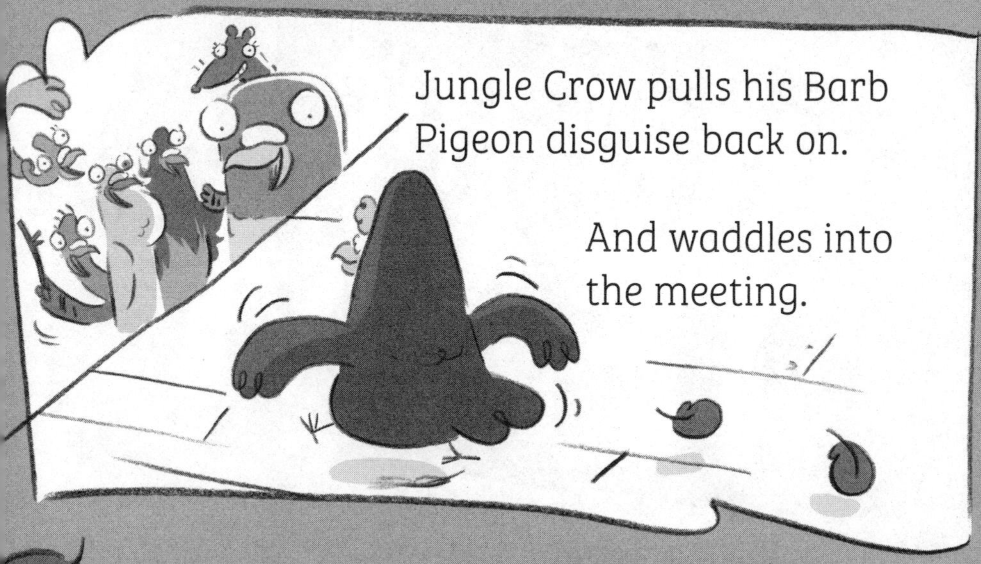
Jungle Crow pulls his Barb Pigeon disguise back on.
And waddles into the meeting.

OH NO! WHAT IS JUNGLE CROW PLANNING?

HOW WILL A GLOBAL NETWORK OF PIGEONS EVEN WORK?

AND WILL ANYONE CLEAN THE DOTS OFF THE CITY?

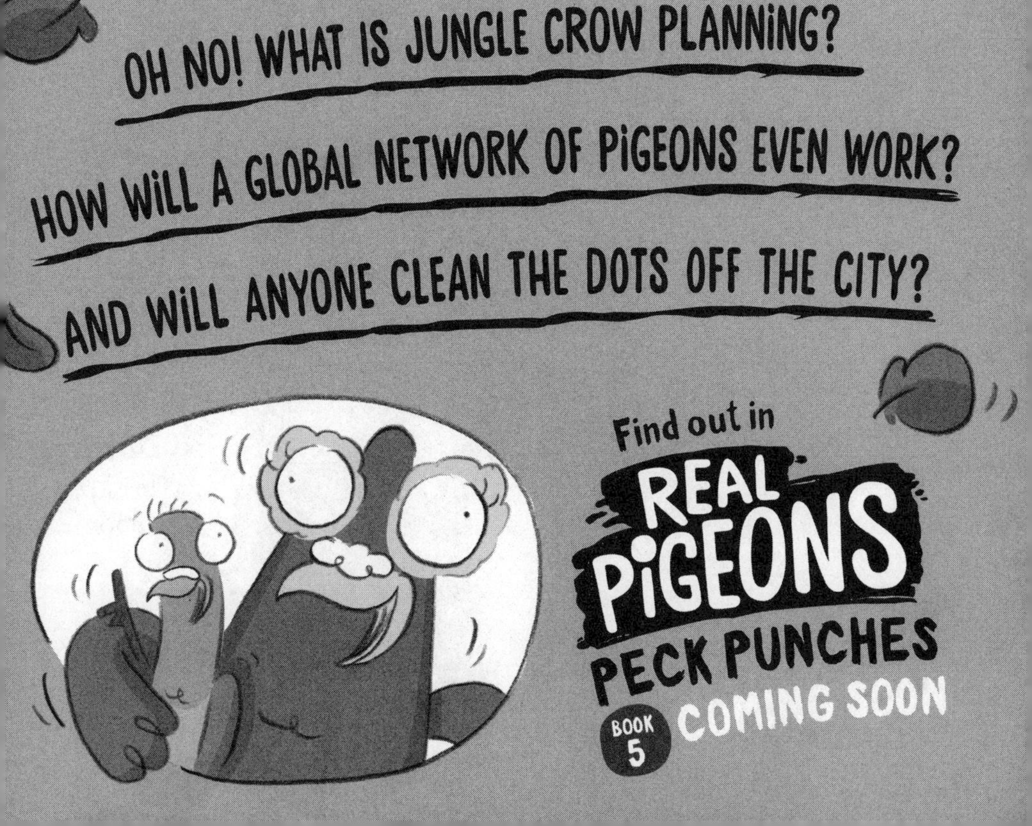

Find out in

REAL PIGEONS PECK PUNCHES

BOOK 5 COMING SOON

MEET THE TEAM

BEN WOOD
awesome illustrator

ANDREW McDONALD
funny author

ANDREW McDONALD is a writer from Melbourne, Australia. He lives with a lovely lady and a bouncy son and enjoys baking his own bread (which he eats down to the last bread crumb—sorry, pigeons!). Visit Andrew at mrandrewmcdonald.com.

BEN WOOD has illustrated more than twenty-five books for children. When Ben isn't drawing, he likes to eat food! His favorite foods include overstuffed burritos, green spaghetti, and big bags of chips! Yum! Visit Ben at benwood.com.au.

FIND OUT MORE ABOUT THE REAL PIGEONS SQUAD AT REALPIGEONS.COM!

DID YOU KNOW

REAL PIGEONS

ARE
REAL-LIFE
PIGEONS?

ROCK PIGEON

The most common pigeon in the world. Gray with two black stripes on each wing. Very good at blending in!

FRILLBACK PIGEON

Known as a "fancy pigeon." Humans have bred them to be covered in curly feathers. These birds don't need to use hair curlers!

TUMBLER PIGEON

Known to tumble somersault while in flight. They fly normally before unexpectedly doing aerial acrobatics.

POUTER PIGEON

The big bubble that looks like a chest is actually called a crop. Pouters store food in their crops before releasing it to their stomachs. Yuck!

HOMING PIGEON

Has the incredible ability to fly long distances and return home from very far away. They were used to deliver letters many years ago.

FIND OUT MORE AT REALPIGEONS.COM!

FRILLBACK PIGEON

Known as a "fancy pigeon." Humans have bred them to be covered in curly feathers. These birds don't need to use hair curlers!

HOMING PIGEON

Has the incredible ability to fly long distances and return home from very far away. They were used to deliver letters many years ago.

TUMBLER PIGEON

Known to tumble or somersault while in flight. They fly normally before unexpectedly doing aerial acrobatics.

POUTER PIGEON

The big bubble that looks like a chest is actually called a crop. Pouters store food in their crops before releasing it to their stomachs. Yuck!

FIND OUT MORE AT
REALPIGEONS.COM!